The Academy

A Female Domination School

Copyright ©2021 Ava Paulson
All rights reserved.

All rights reserved. No part of this publication may be reproduced, distributed, or transmitted in any form or by any means, including photocopying, recording, or other electronic or mechanical methods, without the prior written permission of the author, except in the case of brief quotations embodied in critical reviews and certain other noncommercial uses permitted by copyright law. This is a work of fiction. Any resemblance to actual persons, living or dead, or actual events is purely coincidental. All characters are over the age of eighteen.

Emily

"On behalf of The Academy at West Hills, we are pleased to inform you that your application has been accepted. We wish to offer you our congratulations. As you know, admission to the Academy is highly competitive, which affords us the luxury of selecting only the finest applicants.

We hope that the personal supervision we provide, together with the atmosphere of excellence among our student body, will serve to make your stay here very rewarding—personally, academically, and professionally. We will expect to see you one week before the start of school for room assignments and orientation. In the meantime, please do not hesitate to contact us if you have any questions or concerns.

Sincerely,
The Academy at West Hills Student Admissions Committee"

    Emily held the acceptance letter in her hands, sweeping her hair back behind her ear on the left side as she scanned the letter a second time. She was excited and unsure if she could believe what she was reading. She had just been accepted into the most prestigious private academy in the state, and it appeared as though nothing could prevent her from going. She had cleared the last hurdle, and now held the golden ticket in her hand. Knowing that no one else was home, she let out a full-throated, joyous scream. She danced frantically up and down, shrieking to the ceiling, allowing every bit of tension that had built up due to hope, fear, and anxiety about making it into the Academy dissipate through the manic flailing of her limbs. She noticed that tears had begun streaming down her face, and while such a display of emotion might have otherwise caused her embarrassment, even to herself, for now, she didn't care.

    Later, during dinner, she told her parents, though she presented the news in a far more sober fashion. She was counting on this opportunity so much that she couldn't bear the thought that her parents might not agree to allow her to attend, so it was with some trepidation that she revealed the letter informing her of her acceptance. When her parents signaled their agreement, saying that she had worked hard and deserved the honor of attending, she screamed and danced again—this time, entirely in her head.

Throughout high school, Emily had been a good student, and although she got A's in all of her classes, she never seemed to receive much recognition for being smart. In retrospect, she was grateful for this, as she'd never had to deal with the reputation of being brainy or the nerdy bookworm. But it did irritate her that she sometimes felt invisible.

Emily was naturally quiet, but she felt that she was just more naturally attuned to listening since she found that those who did the most talking were so often wrong and went about being an embarrassment to themselves. She could be shy as well, but she thought of herself as being more cautious than anything. When it came to what she wanted, she certainly didn't demure. This was the case with her application to the Academy. She wanted it, she worked for it, and she got it. It encouraged her, and it inspired her to think of what else she might want.

Emily had decided that she wanted a fresh start and to revise how people saw her. Physically, she hadn't developed in the same time frame that all her friends had, and she still looked kind of mousy, or plain, by her own estimation. She tended to wear her long brown hair pulled back into a ponytail and did little in the way of applying makeup and dressing girly. What she didn't know yet was that she possessed an irresistible quality, an undefinable something that would affect her life going forward. She thought of her eyes as sleepy, and she hadn't come to realize how incredibly beguiling they were to certain boys. And her butt, which she had long been teased about because it was "too big," was now perfectly proportioned, and made her slender body look tremendously sexy. "Sexy" was a word she hadn't ever thought might be applied to her.

She felt excited by the possibilities, and as the summer was winding down, she was not sad that it was ending as much as she was excited for the beginning of the autumn semester. She was glad to have the opportunity to shed her status of being shy, withdrawn, and invisible. She was going to be an entirely new Emily. She would be living on campus, away from home for the first time, and the newness of it and the as-of-yet undiscovered possibilities made her head feel as though she were spinning.

Her parents accompanied her on the ninety-minute drive to campus, and helped her with her suitcases, which she was concerned were inadequate in containing everything she could possibly need for the upcoming months. Her mother reassured her that anything she wanted could be transported to her by car, while her father grunted in disbelief at the tremendous weight of everything she had brought.

"You're just wearing regular clothes, right?"

"Yes, Dad. Why?"

"Because it feels like you have packed enough clothing for the rest of your life!"

"It's not just clothes; I needed to bring other stuff as well."

"I know. Bricks, apparently. And some barbells."

"Thank you for carrying them, Dad," Emily said graciously.

Before the semester officially began, there was a week-long school orientation. The days were spent taking guided tours of the campus and being introduced to each of the professors and the classes they offered. There were core requirements, in addition to which there were electives so that students could tailor their experience and education to their own particular interests.

Emily made a note to herself about Ms. Strickland's photography course. She was impressed with Ms. Strickland, whose tall, thin, imposing figure and no-nonsense manner of speaking impressed her. She was also impressed with her photography. The Academy had the resources to hire extraordinarily talented individuals for each of the disciplines one might study there, and Ms. Strickland's personal work was remarkable.

One of the classes Emily was curious about was one that was required for all incoming students. It had the vague and nonspecific course title of "Rhetoric," and it was taught by a woman named Ms. Harwood. Emily had heard whispers about it, and it seemed to strike fear in the male students, though she had no idea why just yet.

Emily met a few girls from her floor in the dormitory, who she immediately recognized would become friends over the course of the next year. She met Charlotte and Sarah, who were roommates, although the term "roommates" wasn't completely correct. The dorms at the Academy were set up such that two girls shared a suite, each with her own bedroom and bathroom attached.

Charlotte was a classically beautiful girl, Emily thought, with a curvaceous, hourglass figure. She seemed fun, and she laughed a lot and loudly. Sarah, her roommate, was known for acting like a guy, as far as the other girls were concerned. That, and she had a pronounced bubble butt that Charlotte tended to spank like she was a guy on the football team. The two of them together seemed like they were destined to end up in a lot of trouble. *The fun kind of trouble,* Emily thought, observing them.

She also met Juliette and Maya, who were roommates, but they were best friends from high school, so they knew each other very well and had been friends since forever. Juliette was really chill, and she was in the habit of wearing shirts with a plunging neckline to show off her enormous breasts. Emily thought it was funny to watch her interact with the male students because they were strictly prohibited from looking at girls' breasts, so they were always getting in trouble with Juliette. For her part, she delighted in torturing them with the irresistible yet forbidden sight of her cleavage. Maya was really cute, and she was thin and petite, with a golden-brown skin color, long brown hair streaked with natural highlights, and a seemingly irrepressible energy.

Emily had never had a tight little group of friends. She had friends, for sure, but nothing like this little group, which would develop a close-knit cohesiveness throughout the coming year.

Madison

Emily got herself situated in her dorm room, taking the bedroom off to the right side of the suite. She would have a roommate, and all she knew about her was her name.

Madison Leigh appeared later that afternoon, arriving alone and carrying suitcases, boxes, and duffle bags. Madison had long dirty-blond hair and wore a white T-shirt and cutoffs that were shorter than Emily would have been comfortable wearing.

"Hey, I'm Madison," she announced with her hand extended and a friendly smile.

"Hey, nice to meet you," Emily responded, noticing that Madison had a firmer-than-normal handshake.

"I guess we're going to be roommates, so you can call me "M." My friends call me that."

Emily laughed, saying, "My friends call me "Em," so we'll be Em and M."

"That's stupid," Madison replied with a laugh. "We're not doing that."

Emily eyed her new roommate with bemusement, as she helped her bring in a second armload of things from her car.

"It's cool that you have a car," Emily mentioned. "That will help you get around and stuff."

"Yeah, I bought it from my uncle for five hundred bucks, which is pretty cool," Madison replied. "If you ever need a ride, I can help you out."

"Thank you," Emily said in earnest.

She had been concerned about what it might be like having a roommate. She was an only child, so she'd never had to share space before. But Madison seemed like she was going to be pretty easy to get along with.

"So, how are you feeling about the Academy, so far?" Madison inquired once they had gotten everything into the suite and had collapsed onto the sofa. They'd opened a bottle of wine that Madison had brought, which was now poured generously into plastic cups.

"I am not gonna lie about how excited I am," Emily admitted. "I know it makes me sound like a dork, but that's seriously how I feel about it. I mean, academically, it's going to be tough, but that's totally what I want right now."

Madison stared at Emily for a moment, then laughed.

"Are you serious? You are looking forward to the coursework?" Madison asked incredulously.

"Yeah, why is that so funny?" Emily replied suspiciously.

"Oh, no offense, I mean that's totally cool if you're into that. It's just not among my top priorities right now."

"OK, so what are you thinking about, looking forward?"

Madison said nothing for a moment, gazing out the window at the cedar tree on the lawn outside. Then she turned to Emily, looking quite serious.

"What we get to do to the boys," she said, trying to sound casual.

"Oh, that!" Emily replied, laughing.

The Academy at West Hills had been established in 1902 by Margaret Bleeker, a woman with a very peculiar view of gender-related issues. She had intended the school to be an all-girl higher education facility, in the interest of offering a first-class education to young women. A wealthy benefactor, a woman named Violet Harris (according to the story in the school handbook), convinced Ms. Bleeker to admit males as well, by offering her the land and full funding to build the school. Margaret Bleeker (or Maggie B., as the students came to refer to her), consented to the admission of male students, but it prompted her to write a ninety-eight-page handbook that specified a very strict set of rules for all male students. Each of the young men who were admitted was given a copy of the book with the requirement that they read and memorize every page of it.

The Academy at West Hills Handbook for the Male Student, as it was called, could be found in the hands of all the first-year boys. It specified a code of conduct that was fairly exhaustive in its set of requirements and prohibitions. If any of the boys were in violation of any of the rules, they would face rather severe consequences.

Corporal punishment was to be expected for even the slightest deviation from the code of conduct. The school had operated with these rules in place since its inception, and it had come to be that a lot of the girls would familiarize themselves with the rules in order to use them to their advantage. In particular, one of the most important rules was that any disagreement between a male student and a female student would be settled in favor of the female student. Then, due to the fact that there had been a disagreement in the first place, the male student would face punishment. The female student would be given the opportunity to have input regarding the severity of the punishment, such that she would feel that it was fair to her. This punishment would be carried out in the presence of the female student, at the conclusion of which, he would be required to apologize to her. If she accepted the apology, that would be the end of it. If she did not, then another punishment would be determined. This would continue until the female student felt that the male student had undergone a correction in his attitude.

The itinerary for the male students, as opposed to the females, was very different as well. The boys had a lot of physical requirements, beginning with a daily three-mile run at six o'clock in the morning. Since the handbook was written in 1902, when boys generally were nude for swimming classes, all of the young men were required to be naked for any physical activity. Following the run, they were required to shower, but the shower facility was located along the outer wall on the side of the gymnasium building. There was a large area with a wooden deck, and showerheads placed every meter along the wall of the building. This regimen was carried out during the winter months as well, as the cold air was good for the male body, according to Margaret Bleeker.

At all other times, aside from physical exercise, the boys had a prescribed uniform, which consisted of a white long-sleeved shirt, a necktie, dark-colored trousers, a leather belt, and black leather dress shoes. A sport coat was required for all extracurricular events.

"I think the boys look sharp in their uniforms," Emily observed as she and Madison were out taking a walk around campus, familiarizing themselves with the layout.

Madison laughed.

"Yeah, you would say that. I am just annoyed that getting up at six in the morning is out of the question."

"What happens at six in the morning?" Emily asked.

Madison just rolled her eyes and shook her head.

"You'll find out," she replied.

As they walked along the curved, paved pathway, every male student they encountered stepped to one side and more-or-less came to attention.

"I'm not sure how I feel about the fact that the boys do that," Emily mused. "I mean, it's nice to be able to walk without having to move out of anyone's way, and it feels like a show of respect, but it's a little unnerving too. I've just never seen it before, and it seems weird."

"Hmm ... I love it," Madison replied. "Seeing young, hot men come to attention is like an aphrodisiac."

"Yeah, I noticed that there is an inordinate number of really hot guys. What's up with that?"

"Well, for one, the school can be very selective about the students they admit. I have heard that the interviews the boys go through to get in are pretty difficult. And also, the really rigorous physical routine that they require of all the guys means that they all end up in really good shape. Like this one here," Madison said, gesturing ahead along the path.

Emily turned her attention in the direction that Madison was pointing, and her mouth fell open. Off the path, on a circular, brick-lined slab of concrete in the middle of a large, grass-covered courtyard, stood one of the male students. He was standing at attention with his arms up and his hands placed behind his head. He was also completely naked.

"Oh my gosh!" Emily exclaimed. "What is going on there?"

"Ha!" Madison laughed. "You really *are* new here, aren't you?"

"What—you're new here too!"

"Yeah, but unlike you, I have read the handbook for the male students. This is one of the traditional punishments, and this little circle of pavement has existed since the school was founded. It's one of the places where punishments are carried out, and usually the guy has to remain standing there for a certain length of time. Sometimes just a few hours, but it might be longer," Madison explained. "C'mon," she said as she began walking across the grass, headed directly toward the naked male student.

"What? Surely, you're not going to ..." Emily trailed off, as she realized the futility of her words.

Clearly, Madison *was* going to.

Madison walked up and stood directly in front of him. His eyes were staring straight ahead, and he did not move.

"What are you here for?" Madison asked.

"I am being punished for speaking out of turn, Miss," he replied.

Margaret Bleeker had implemented, among her hundreds of other rules, the rule that all male students address all females as *ma'am,* which was one of the few rules that had eventually been changed, since the girls at the school generally hated being called *ma'am*. And so, at the insistence of the female student body, this was changed to the honorific *miss*.

"I see," Madison replied as she began circling his body, looking him up and down. "Classes haven't even started yet. You must have fucked up pretty good. What's your name?"

"My name is James Brooke, Miss," he replied.

Emily stood upon the edge of the circular pavement, watching in fascination as her new roommate grilled the naked guy as he stood at attention.

"You have a nice ass, James," Madison commented as she gave his smooth, muscular butt a pinch.

"Thank you, Miss; this is my second year here, so—"

"Did I ask you that?" Madison snapped. She came around to stand in front of him again. "Speaking out of turn, right? That's why you are here? It seems like you have a lot to learn."

She drew her middle finger back with her thumb and flicked him surprisingly hard across the head of his penis. He winced, but he did not flinch. His dick swung back and forth from the impact, but no other part of his body moved from its position.

Wow, that is one big dick, Emily thought to herself.

"How long are you being made to stand here?" Madison asked.

"Until five o'clock, Miss," James replied.

Madison turned to look at the campus clock tower across the courtyard from where they were standing.

"Make it six," she declared. "If I see you leaving a minute earlier, I will report you."

She gave him another flick across the head of his penis.

"Understand?"

"Yes, I understand. Thank you, Miss," James replied.

Emily was surprised to see that he was starting to become hard.

"Well, then," Madison said, crossing her arms while observing his state of arousal. "You are so lucky I don't report you for *that*," she stated, indicating his now semi-erect penis. "Just consider it part of your punishment that you now have to stand here fully exposed with an erection. See you later, James."

Madison turned to Emily with a big smile on her face, then bit her lip to keep from laughing.

As they departed the circular area, Emily looked over in wonder at her new roommate.

"That was, um, impressive. But what did he mean when he said, "This is my second year," right before you," and Emily laughed while saying it, "flicked him on his penis?"

"Oh, yeah, it's that the boys have this physical regimen, and they all end up in really good shape. By their second year, they've developed really nice bodies."

"Oh, right. So, then, is he on the swim team, or something? I mean, because he was all shaved."

Madison shook her head.

"You really didn't read the handbook, did you? It's a requirement. Maggie B. had a thing about body hair, so all the boys are completely shaved, which is fucking awesome."

"He did look really nice that way. I've just never seen that before."

"Well, I imagine you are going to see a lot of things you've never seen before," Madison replied, laughing.

"Why do they come here, then? I mean, why do boys come to the Academy if all of that is expected of them?"

"Well, it looks great on their resumé, for one. And for some, they end up enrolled here without knowing the full extent of what will happen to them. And for some of the guys," Madison lowered her voice, "it's court ordered."

"What? You mean, like, they're criminals?"

"No, not exactly that. More like, they got to a point where it was either going to be *this* or something far worse."

"Wow. Well, I look forward to seeing what all is going to happen," Emily admitted.

"Like I told you, this is going to be a lot of fun."

Ms. Harwood

A few days later, classes officially began, and Emily's first class was the legendary Ms. Harwood's Rhetoric class. Emily took a seat in the first row, in front of the teacher's desk. This position in the classroom, which she customarily chose for herself, was beneficial to her studies because it afforded her an unobstructed view of the chalkboard and any other presentational materials. As it would turn out, it allowed her a singular view of something else.

Ms. Harwood was very, very strict, and when it came to disciplining her students, she was unrivaled. Corporal punishment was embraced as a method for conditioning the male students, and she was somewhat famous for her insistence on its application.

Historically it was as often as once a week that one of the boys in the class was called to the front of the class. It was, without exception, an electrifying moment. All of the students in the class would go silent as the boy would surrender himself to his fate, blushing with embarrassment as he dutifully made his way to the front of the class to stand beside her desk.

He would then be obligated to unbuckle his belt, unbutton and unzip his trousers, and then slide his pants, along with his underwear, down to his ankles. Then, he was to lean forward and place his hands upon her desk.

Miss Harwood would draw out the punishment, counting on the humiliation of being exposed to assist in modifying the boy's behavior. She would leave him in this position while she questioned him about what he had done and whether or not he thought he'd acted appropriately. Inevitably, she led each boy to the logical conclusion that the only possible outcome was that he would receive his allotment of strokes from the long birch rod that she kept mounted on the wall behind her desk.

On the very first day of class, as Ms. Harwood was calling out the names of each student registered for her class, the door flew open, and a young man hurried into the room and quickly found an open desk. He had just set down his belongings when he noticed the teacher silently staring at him. He swallowed hard. He looked as though he were about to speak—most likely to offer some apology for being late—when Ms. Harwood addressed him.

"What is your name?" she asked, her voice terrifying in its tone of unquestioned authority.

"Michael," the student replied, his voice strained. "Michael Woods."

"Come to the front of the class, Michael," she demanded, her voice like artic air.

Michael stood up, his face a shade of crimson, and made his way to the front of the class. He stood where Ms. Harwood indicated.

"Assume the position," Ms. Harwood brusquely commanded.

Emily was just four feet away, uniquely positioned to watch the show that was about to begin.

Michael unbuckled his belt, unbuttoned and unzipped his pants, then slid them down to his ankles. He placed both hands on the desk, arms straight, and arched his back to present his bare butt for punishment (this posture was described in the handbook).

Ms. Harwood didn't mind when the boys took their time in assuming the position. In fact, she felt that this was a significant part of the punishment, and the longer the boy took in doing it, the more torturous it was for him.

Emily sat transfixed, watching Michael. Once he had assumed the prescribed position, Ms. Harwood unceremoniously pulled his shirttail up his back, exposing him from mid-torso down.

But the humiliating exposure was just the beginning. Ms. Harwood reprimanded him until he was obligated to ask her, politely, if she would give him the punishment he deserved. When he had shown this adjustment in attitude, she brought forth the dreaded birch rod. She placed it against his smooth, rounded cheeks. She asked him to request the number of strokes of the rod that he thought was appropriate (Ten was generally a safe answer, but a more severe punishment was in store if the number requested was thought to be too low).

Throughout this ordeal, Emily enjoyed the guilty pleasure of seeing him completely exposed. She loved the anticipation, watching how nervous he was while waiting for the birch rod to land upon his exposed backside. She tried to take it all in, from the sight of his nakedness to the sound the rod made, to the gasp he emitted when the first stroke landed. She found that she particularly enjoyed the little bounce his dick made when the rod made contact.

All of the boys came to learn that Ms. Harwood had a sadistic streak and seemed to enjoy making the punishment hurt. She would pause between each stroke, allowing its effect to sink in. The student was required to not only count each stroke but thank her as well. When she was finished, she would have him remain in place for a minute more as she warned him that further misbehavior would be more severely punished.

When she had finished with Michael's punishment, Ms. Harwood had him stand and turn toward the class to apologize for wasting everyone's time. Both his face and his ass were bright red as he addressed the class. Emily found that she couldn't help but stare at his dick as he offered his apology. And then he was allowed to pull up his pants and return to his seat.

"My gosh," Emily said in wonder to Madison later that day. "It was so unbelievably humiliating for him."

"Oh, boo-hoo," Madison replied in mock concern, then laughed.

"No, I'm not saying that because I felt sorry for him," Emily protested. "I'm saying that because I really liked it. It was just so fascinating to watch him standing there being totally humiliated."

"See? I told you it was going to be fun," Madison said with a broad smile.

Ms. Strickland

Emily felt a nervous, excited energy as she made her way across campus for her first day of Photography 1, which was taught by Ms. Strickland. It was Emily's one elective in addition to the core requirements which made up the rest of her schedule. When she arrived at the Creative Arts building, she found the photography studio by following the smell of the chemicals. Ms. Strickland was old school, literally, and had all of her students shoot and develop film.

"You can learn the digital photography shit later," she would say, surprising Emily with her use of profanity.

Ms. Strickland was a formidable figure, and she spoke directly and was known to be very frank in her assessments of her students' work. She was also known for enlisting her male students to pose for her in her own, personal work.

"I believe that you should have an opportunity to view my work, since you will be taking my class," Ms. Strickland said in her loud, thin voice. She directed the students to the wall, upon which she had displayed a series of photographs. They were large-format print photos, and they were primarily black-and-white with bold, red-colored areas.

"My interest, currently, is to reinterpret the fairy tales we are all familiar with, and in this series, I have focused on 'Little Red Riding Hood.'"

The photos had a surreal quality, featuring a young female walking through the woods, her red coat being the primary focus, as it was a deep crimson, whereas the rest of the photo was essentially black-and-white. The wolf character was represented by a young male, who wore a fairly realistic mask, which Emily thought was actually kind of terrifying, and was otherwise nude. One of the deviations from the original story was that in the second-to-last photo, Little Red Riding Hood is seen slamming her knee between the legs of the guy playing the wolf.

"I have a question," one of the male students asked after the class had spent a few minutes examining the series of photos.

"And what is your question?" Ms. Strickland asked.

"In the photo where the wolf is getting kneed, um, between the legs, how did you achieve that effect? I mean, it looks really convincing."

Ms. Strickland stared at the student for a moment, saying nothing.

"I had the model playing Red knee him in the balls," she said dryly. "Would you like to have that demonstrated?"

"Um, no, I just—"

"No, you ask a stupid question in my class, and you get an answer. What is your name?"

"David," he replied, his voice sounding small.

"David, come to the front of the class, and stand here," she said, pointing to the floor.

David reluctantly got to his feet and walked to the front of the class.

"Remove your pants for this demonstration," she said as she searched the room. "You. What is your name?"

"Emily."

"Emily, please come here."

Emily went to stand next to David, who was now wearing a shirt and underwear.

"Take your underwear off as well, David," Ms. Strickland instructed. "We want to see what is happening, and Emily needs to see what she is doing."

David hesitantly took off his underwear, but the tails of his shirt still covered him in front.

"Oh, right. Take off your shirt as well," Ms. Strickland said impatiently.

David looked like he might be sick to his stomach. His face was flushed bright red, and he even looked like he might start crying.

Emily was still a bit unsure of what was going to happen, and she didn't love having to stand up in front of the class, but she thought David's reaction was a bit much. Oh, just get on with it, David, she thought to herself.

Once David was completely naked, Ms. Strickland directed Emily's attention to the photograph in question.

"If you will, please, Emily, do it precisely like that."

Emily examined the model's position in the photograph, then turned toward David. She placed her hands on David's shoulders, and never having done this before, she hesitated, uncertain of herself.

"Go ahead, Emily," Ms. Strickland said.

Emily brought her leg back as David tried to steel himself. She sent her knee up between his legs and slammed it against his balls. She surprised herself with how hard she'd pounded him, and was intrigued by the feeling of his balls being smashed between her bare knee and his body. David involuntarily cried out and promptly fell to his knees before her. Emily was also surprised by the feeling that came over her, watching David crumple to the floor, his naked body wracked with agonizing pain. She had to bite her lip to keep from laughing, and she simultaneously experienced a powerful sensation that came in a rush. She realized that she was aroused, and suddenly became aware that she was still standing in front of a classroom of students. One of the girls in the class applauded.

"OK, David," Ms. Strickland announced, "so if you still want to know how I captured that moment in the photograph, I can tell you that I had the female model repeat that action many more times until I was able to get exactly the right moment and the right reaction. Are you still confused? Do you need another demonstration?"

"No," David replied, his voice reduced to a hoarse whisper.

"I didn't think so. Now stand up and thank Emily for her part in this demonstration."

The First Time

"So, I kneed a guy in the balls in class today," Emily said, trying to sound casual. She was sitting in the large armchair in the suite, her feet tucked up underneath her.

Madison was lying on the sofa. They were both taking a break from classwork.

"Good for you!" Madison replied. "Did he cry?"

"No, but he did drop to his knees in front of the class."

"Is this a, uh, ballbusting class that I don't know about?"

"No," Emily replied, laughing. "It's my photography class, which I think is going to be really good. The teacher is this amazing lady who is incredibly talented."

"Oh. I guess I fucked up by taking Geography, Cartology, and the World of Tomorrow."

"Oh, yeah, that sounds like a mistake," Emily replied, laughing.

She then became quiet as she pondered a thought.

"Can I tell you a secret?" Emily asked, her voice soft and vulnerable.

"A secret? Do tell," Madison implored.

"Well, I'm a, I mean, I've never, um—"

"No," Madison interrupted, incredulous. "No, you can't possibly be saying—"

"Well, uh, it's just that—"

"You have got to be kidding me! Are you truly telling me that—"

"I'm a virgin," Emily blurted out. "There. I said it."

"Wow. I mean, yeah, OK, there's nothing wrong with that; I don't judge. Is it for, like, is there some specific reason why, or anything? I mean, you're super-cool, you're cute as shit, you've got a sweet pair of tits, and a sexy-ass … um, ass."

"Uh, thank you, I guess, but, no, it's just that … I think that I just got this reputation when I was younger. Everyone just thought I was this, you know, Goody Two-shoes."

"Oh, yeah, and look at you now, you busted a guys' balls in class this morning," Madison teased.

"Ha-ha, shut up!" Emily replied, laughing. "Here's the thing, though. And I am admitting all this to you under strictest confidence."

"Lockbox," Madison interrupted. "I'm a lockbox."

"OK, well, the thing is that I liked it. I mean, I'm not into David, or anything, but seeing him naked, and then, um, ramming my knee into his balls, it kind of turned me on. Is that weird?"

"No, not at all."

"And that guy, I think his name is James? I'm still kind of fascinated with that, um, situation. And then, oh my gosh, Ms. Harwood's class? I have seen quite a few guys now have to take a punishment, and I have seen so many guys naked and in compromising positions!"

"Woah, slow down there, girl, you're going to overheat!" Madison said, laughing. "And since you mention him, I am totally going to be taking advantage of that guy named James. I decided that he is going to be my bitch-boy."

Emily laughed.

"What do you do with a bitch-boy?"

"Whatever you fucking want," Madison declared, laughing at the thought.

"So tell me, do you mean that you have absolutely no experience with boys?" Madison inquired.

"Well, no. I mean, yeah, kind of, but there was one thing that happened."

Emily thought about the closest she'd gotten to having something happen with a boy. She had been standing in an alcove off of the main hallway, making out with a guy she had a crush on. Suddenly, she felt something that surprised her. With little warning, there was something hard pressing against her lower abdomen. Silly, Emily thought to herself. It's his penis. Boys have them, and sometimes they get hard. There were two things that she found curious, however. *We're just kissing*, she thought to herself. *Does just kissing me make his penis hard?* And also, it felt ... big. Really big. It felt as if it would hurt him, the way that it was straining against his denim pants. *Can it rip right through his jeans?* she wondered. She almost laughed out loud at that thought, laughing at herself more than anything, but then she let all thoughts go and just let this one rapturous moment consume her, wrapped in his arms.

"Worst timing possible," she whispered aloud as she heard voices approaching. She felt self-conscious all of a sudden, and he let her go as she whipped around to face the small group of students who had interrupted their private moment. Happily, they seemed to be more preoccupied with their pointless chatter than with whatever she might be doing. It immediately occurred to her that she had left her guy in an embarrassing state, with an erection in his pants, and because she felt she'd been the cause of it, she felt obligated to help conceal it. To that end, she backed up against him, so that no one could see around her. She could feel it pressed against her ass, and it was all that she could do to maintain a straight face under the circumstances. For what reason never she found out, but nothing further happened with that particular boy, and it was shortly afterward that she packed up to start the year at the Academy.

Her lack of experience drew her closer to her roommate, Madison, who seemed to be much wiser and more experienced with boys and how to handle them. Emily recognized that she had a lot to learn.

"I guess you have a lot more experience with boys?" Emily asked.

"How dare you!" Madison said, then laughed. "But yeah."

Madison sat thinking, observing Emily. She wondered how she could be so innocent and so inexperienced.

"So, the first time," Madison began, having decided to tell the story of her first encounter with a boy, "there was this one, brief moment where I was standing in the hallway at school, talking to a couple of my friends, and something caught my eye. It happened so fast, but it was as though time slowed down, like, slower than I'd ever experienced before. I saw this guy standing there, and he was talking to a friend of his. I kind of had a crush on this guy. His name was Devon. Anyway, he was wearing a pair of sweatpants and a T-shirt because it was either before or after gym class, and he was absentmindedly scratching the side of his body, which pulled the hem of his shirt upward, exposing about half of his upper body above the waistline of his sweats. I could see his abs, and his sweats were set low, so my eyes were drawn to seeing this part of him all exposed."

Emily smiled at her roommate, imagining her drawn like a magnet to the sight of naked boy parts.

"I could see his navel, but it also occurred to me in that moment that he was looking at me. I noticed one of his friends approaching him from behind with a maniacal look in his eye. He was laughing as his hands extended outward, and he grabbed Devon's sweatpants on either side of his hips with both hands and yanked them down. Time practically ground to a halt. I watched, unable to do anything but stare as the two handfuls of fabric were whipped downward, and it struck me that between the two downward-moving fists were not only his sweats, but his underwear as well. I watched as the elastic waistband slid down and made his dick bounce as it popped out, and it was fully exposed to me alone. I forgot about the conversation I was having with my friends, who were facing me, unaware of what was happening. I saw everything in that moment, as his sweats had been almost instantaneously relocated around his ankles."

Madison laughed at this point, having painted the image for Emily in such great detail. Emily had to laugh as well, mostly due to the infectiousness of Madison's laugh.

"When I thought about it later," Madison continued, "I thought mostly about the fact that during this millisecond, he'd done nothing. It had happened so quickly that it hadn't even occurred to him yet to be surprised. Instead, he simply stood there with his shirt pulled up a bit and his sweatpants pulled down completely, and he was looking at me. The moment was also remarkable in that having witnessed it, I could replay it in my mind as often as I liked. And I could pause it. I could freeze this moment and just stand there observing Devon having just been completely exposed to me in the middle of the hallway in the middle of the day. Everyone else was busy with their own thoughts and conversations in between classes, and in the center of it, this guy I had a crush on was standing there almost completely naked for me to examine at will.

"Allowing time to creep forward, very slowly, I could observe the look on his face as the realization of what had just happened dawned on him. I could pause the memory again to savor the moment when, though he was still standing before me, still so naked, he became aware of the fact that he was completely exposed to me. I freeze this moment and examine it carefully. I study the look on his face. I see so many conflicting emotions. First, and perhaps most importantly, I can see that he is now aware that I am seeing him, and specifically, I can see everything. All of his secrets have been exposed. It is as though he has been stripped for me alone to view. And I know as well that there is absolutely nothing that he can do about it. It has already happened, and he is now mine to observe in freeze-frame."

Emily was somewhat taken aback by the detail with which Madison had mentally recorded this brief encounter, but she was also fascinated in listening to her roommate's recollection of the event.

"So, the second thing is, I can see the transition from him realizing what has happened to him having to do something about it. I wondered, thinking about it later, *Did he hesitate?* Obviously, his motivation was to cover himself since he was fully exposed in the middle of the hallway, and so he did reach down to grab ahold of his sweats to pull them back up, but did he do it as quickly as he was able? Or was there not, in fact, just the slightest bit of hesitation due to the fact that he liked the part where he was standing naked before me?

"When I had an opportunity to ask him about it later, he blushed, and admitted that, well, maybe he did hesitate just slightly. But in the moment, even though I had slowed down time until the second hand on the clock was barely moving, still, he did actually grab his sweats and yank them back up. But even then, he watched me the entire time, and I saw that the waistband of the sweats slid up his thighs and caused his dick to flip upward against his body as it went past. And then the moment was over. Except for one last thing: He looked up, blushing, and made eye contact with me. His dick was now in an upward position in his sweats—the outline of it, clearly visible to me—and he certainly wasn't going to reach into his sweatpants and adjust it at that point. Since his friend had already taken the opportunity to run away, laughing as he took off down the hall, he remained in place, and gave me a questioning look: *Did that really just happen?* His eyes met mine, but then they lowered, and I could see that he had an erection. He a couple of books and a folder in one hand, but he didn't cover himself right away. I could see that he was holding them to the side. He wanted me to look. I had just seen him naked, and now he wanted me to see him hard.

"OK, so now it gets good," Madison said, leaning forward. "Three weeks later, I did see him standing before me, fully naked and completely hard, in the basement of my house. I presented to him the logic that since I had already seen him with his pants down, he might as well take off his clothes. So he began taking off his clothes. When he was naked, it was as though we had returned to that moment in the hallway. Only now, he was in no hurry to put his clothes back on. And I had no reason not to stare. I watched his cock get hard. And I stared. He was so fucking big!" Madison exclaimed.

Emily smiled. *Of course he was,* she thought.

"I wasn't ready to do anything else, so I told him to jerk himself off in front of me. Now, what surprised me as I watched, was that it wasn't over quickly. I had heard that boys don't take long to come, but I began to be aware that he wasn't going to finish anytime soon. Instead, he kept stroking his cock, his eyes on me the entire time. I watched intently as he approached orgasm, but instead of coming, he slowed down a bit and continued to play with himself while I watched. I realized that he was intentionally trying to make it last as long as possible. I had him promise me that this would happen again, and he readily agreed. And then he brought himself to orgasm, and I watched him come."

Madison was still for a moment, then turned her gaze to Emily.

"Why did I tell you that story?" she asked.

"I don't really know, I guess we were talking about, you know, the first time or whatever.

"Right. So, I really like big fucking dicks on cute boys was my point."

"Got it," Emily replied, happy to have such a cool roommate.

James

The next day, Madison entered the boys' dormitory on a mission. She was amused by the fact that the dorm was so open. The girls' dorm was keycard protected, with security staff on duty. Male students were only allowed in when escorted by a female student, and each of the girls had a private bedroom in their own suite. Conversely, the boys' dorm was open, there were two male students to each room, and the rooms themselves didn't even have doors.

Madison made her way down the hall, looking at each of the plaques on the doorframes, which listed the room number and the names of the boys in each room. Finally, she found what she was looking for.

"James Brooke," she said to herself, then entered the room.

When the two guys in the room became aware of her presence, they both jumped up and stood at attention.

"James?" Madison called out.

"Yes, Miss?" James replied, turning slightly toward her but remaining at attention.

"Oh, good, I was hoping to find you. I wanted to give you the opportunity to ask me out on a date," Madison stated in her remarkably forward manner.

"Oh," James replied, sounding flustered.

"What? Do you have a girlfriend?" she asked.

"Um, no."

"Is he your girlfriend?" she asked, gesturing to James's roommate, who remained at attention.

"No, Miss," James replied with an amused smile.

"OK, then."

"It's that I was unaware that you wanted ... I mean, sure, yes. Absolutely. Would you do me the honor of going out on a date with me?" James managed.

"I thought you'd never ask," Madison replied—her delivery, comically sweet. "One thing to get straight though," she said as she took a step closer. She reached out, unzipped his pants, and pulled his penis out. She wrapped her hand firmly around his balls and his dick and looked him in the eyes.

"If you want to date me, then this is mine," she said while giving him a firm squeeze. "Do you understand?"

"Yes, Miss" he replied.

Madison laughed.

"Oh, right. My name is Madison."

"Yes, Miss Madison," James replied.

He was beginning to get an erection when suddenly she removed her hand and turned to make her departure.

"Friday at 6 p.m., main courtyard," she said over her shoulder.

The Plan

Charlotte made her way to the boys' dormitory, in search of her roommate, Sarah. Sarah had taken one of the part-time jobs that were available to the students, and she was currently in the middle of her shift as a shower attendant. As per the rules established by Margaret Bleeker, the school's founder, boys were only allowed to shower when supervised, as she was very concerned about whatever shenanigans they might get up to if left to their own devices. Charlotte found the shower room at the end of the hall on the first floor, and knew she was in the right place since the room did not have a door, and the showers themselves were simply showerheads mounted to the wall. Anyone walking by would have a clear view of each one of the boys.

Charlotte found her roommate sitting on a barstool behind a little desk with a slanted top, on which she had a clipboard. She was dividing her attention between the boys in the shower and a text she was reading for her Political Science course.

"Hey, Sarah," Charlotte called out as she entered.

Sarah looked up from her book.

"Oh, hey, Charlotte. What's up?"

"I had something I wanted to run by you," she began.

Just at that point, one of the young men approached Sarah's desk.

"Do you mind?" Charlotte snapped, looking at the boy who stood, dripping wet, waiting to ask for one of the towels that Sarah had on the shelves behind her. "I'm trying to talk to my friend."

"Oh, just let me get it over with, Charlotte," Sarah said. "It will be annoying if he just stands here the whole time."

Sarah scanned the boy's body up and down, then told him to turn around, which he did.

"OK," she pronounced, and handed him a towel.

He expressed his gratitude to both of them and departed quickly.

"What was that about?" Charlotte inquired.

"Oh, I have to check to make sure they are both clean and well-shaved. You know Maggie B. had a thing about boys with body hair."

"Oh, right," Charlotte recalled. "You have a weird job. Anyway, I had an idea, and I couldn't wait to run it by you."

"All ears," Sarah replied.

"OK. So, you know how I had to walk all the way over here just now—like you do every day, I suppose?"

"Every other day, but go on."

"OK, well, now I could walk all the way over, and I could walk in and observe any of the guys here, but this is just a small selection of the male student body."

Sarah suppressed a smile at the phrase "male student body."

"And of course, I could get my ass out of bed at six in the morning to watch the guys running or those showering at the athletic building."

"Sure," Sarah replied, as she had done so herself.

"And a number of the guys are going to be available to view during various punishments or whatever, but here's the thing."

Sarah was encouraged that Charlotte seemed to be closing in on her point.

"There is no convenient way for me, as a student, to view all of the boys that I want, and even then, I don't have the full set of information that I might like to have."

At that point, another young man warily approached Sarah.

"Oh, fuck," Charlotte exclaimed, exasperated by the interruption.

"I apologize, Miss," the boy said.

"Hey, Charlotte, check this out," Sarah said, pointing at the boy's penis.

Charlotte looked, and noticed that he was uncircumcised.

"Oh my God!" she exclaimed. "I've never seen one up close!"

"Watch this," Sarah said, and turning to the boy standing before them, ordered, "Make it hard."

"Yes, Miss," he replied, and began stroking himself.

"Oh, that's so fucking weird," Charlotte observed, watching his foreskin slide back and forth.

Within moments, he was fully erect.

"Stop," Sarah directed.

"Oh, interesting," Charlotte commented. "He doesn't look uncircumcised when he's hard."

"I know, right?" Sarah responded.

She handed a towel to the young man, but raised her hand, pointing a finger in his face.

"No playing with your penis, you understand? That was for demonstration purposes only."

"Yes, Miss, I understand," he replied.

"You understand what?" Sarah replied, her voice icy in its tone.

"I am not to play with my penis, Miss," he replied.

Sarah said nothing in reply, simply pointed at the door, indicating that he was to leave after toweling off.

After he had departed, Charlotte turned to Sarah.

"What is his name? He is cute, and that was one big dick, in spite of the fact that he is uncircumcised."

"His name is Antony," Sarah replied. "He's nice, I guess."

"Well, see? That's what I was talking about. What we need is, like, a database of all the guys, so that all the girls can find out stuff, like what each of the guys is really like, and, um, what he looks like hard—because I want to know shit like that."

"Well, OK, I'm down. It seems like a good idea. I guess it's just a logistics thing, like, how we make it happen."

"I have that part figured out," Charlotte said with a wink.

At this point, there was only one guy left in the shower, and it was approaching the end of Sarah's shift. The last guy came up to get his towel, and Sarah suddenly sat up straight in her chair.

"What's this?" she asked, pointing at a bit of stubble in his pubic region.

"Um ..." he said meekly.

"Go fucking shave it, Dick," she demanded.

He turned to do just that as Charlotte laughed.

"It that really his name?" she asked.

"His name is Richard, so I call him Dick. I think it suits him."

When Dick returned, shaved smooth, Sarah made no move to grab a towel.

"Position," she intoned flatly.

Dick immediately placed his arms up and his hands behind his head. Sarah slapped him across the balls. He made a whimpering sound, which made Charlotte laugh.

"Do you mind if I have one?" Charlotte asked.

"Not at all," Sarah replied.

Charlotte stepped forward and gave him a hard slap with her palm flat, which practically brought him to his knees.

"Oh, nice!" Sarah offered as a compliment.

She then stepped forward and slammed her fist into his balls, which fully dropped him to his knees.

Charlotte laughed, and proclaimed, "See, Dick, that's why you need to follow the rules. Otherwise, my friend here will deliver a much-deserved punishment."

Once Dick recovered, he issued an apology and expressed his gratitude to the both of them for his correction. Following that, he was allowed to stand up, and he was excused.

"OK, well, I'll get some of the girls together, and we'll launch this plan," Charlotte concluded.

"I am looking forward to it," Sarah replied.

The Letter

"Hey, you got a letter. Here," Madison suddenly remembered, handing Emily a handwritten envelope.

Madison was lying on the couch in the suite, trying to think of anything that might be more interesting than her biology textbook. Emily tended to focus on her academic work so completely that Madison sometimes felt alone in the room.

"That's odd," Emily observed, pulling her attention from the essay she was writing on her laptop. She wondered who might have sent a handwritten letter as she slit open the envelope.

>Dear Emily,
>
>I wanted to write to you about what happened on Friday afternoon. Given Ms. Harwood's attitude about maintaining order in her classroom, it was only a matter of time before I found myself walking up to the front of the class for her famous "drop your pants to your ankles" punishment.
>
>I have seen the other guys in class dutifully pulling their pants down and bending over her desk, and how embarrassed they looked to be doing it, but I couldn't have imagined that it is so much more humiliating than

that. This is not to say that I was embarrassed about your seeing me that way, and that is the reason I am writing to you. As you are aware, I had an erection. I don't know if this has happened with other guys in class. But I wanted to tell you that it was because of you that I got hard. The fact that you could see me with my pants pulled down, getting whipped with the birch rod, turned me on so much that I got hard in spite of the circumstances. So I wanted to write to you to explain. It certainly wasn't because of Ms. Harwood. It was because at that moment, your eyes upon me allowed me to completely focus upon you, as though it was for you alone that I was displayed, and each of the twenty strokes of the birch rod were for you as well. That is what caused me to become hard, which compounded the situation, because then you were watching me get punished with an erection, which made me even more focused on the fact that you were watching me. It was such a relief to realize that you were there with me in that incredibly embarrassing moment. Having you there, witnessing everything that was happening to me, made it not only bearable, but I was actually able to enjoy it. That might sound weird, but it is difficult to explain just how arousing your presence was in that moment.

And so, I wanted to write to you to ask you for something. It makes me nervous just writing it. But here it goes. I want you to whip me. I know that is an enormous favor I am asking of you. I realize that I would have to earn it, which I am prepared to do. However you like. I will do anything you ask. And there is no limit to what you may ask. What I want in exchange is to assume whatever position you choose, with my pants down (or off, if you want), and for you to whip me. Also, you may decide where this will take place, should you agree to do this favor for me. The only thing that I will ask is that if you decide to do this, is that you whip me hard, and for a long time. As I said, I will do anything you ask of me in exchange. You have every right to ask for anything you want.

I am aware that you could decide to show this note to Ms. Harwood, which would get me in a huge amount of trouble and would result in my being punished even more in front of you and the rest of the class. However, I have decided to take the risk, hoping that you decide not to do that, and instead, give me the opportunity to earn a punishment from you. At the same time, I send you this letter with the understanding that you might decide to show it to one of your girlfriends. I am aware that girls tend to talk to one another about really private stuff. I mean, I discovered at some point that all of the girls in the class know how big or how small each of the boys' dicks are from having seen them during their punishment. And since I unavoidably had my first punishment on Friday, it is only a matter of time until they all know about me as well.

Anyway, I wouldn't mind if you decided to share with a girlfriend at school the fact that I want to be whipped by you. While it might be embarrassing to me, it would still be an honor for me to have you even consider it. Also, to clarify, though the standard punishment in class is across the desk, with pants and underwear pulled down, that is not necessarily the way that you would do it. Rather, it would be entirely up to you, and it could be any way that you want—however you want me to be positioned, wearing whatever you say, and wherever you decide. I could suggest that we go to the old barn, the one that is a mile or so back in the woods. Not very many people go there, so it's possible that we could be completely alone for some length of time. But that is just a suggestion. The decision would be yours to make.

Thank you for considering this favor I am asking of you. Please think about what you might want me to do to earn the right to be whipped by you. I will do whatever you say.

Sincerely yours,
Neil

"Oh my God! What the actual fuck?" Emily blurted out.

"What is it?" Madison asked, sounding alarmed.

"Read," Emily replied, handing her the letter.

"Oh my God! What the actual fuck?" Madison cried out a minute later.

"I know, right? Fucking Neil."

"What are you going to do? Because you should definitely report him."

"Yeah, I mean, maybe. He did ask me not to, but ..."

"Ha! Who gives a shit what he wants? Although ..."

"What?"

"Well," Madison sat up, clearly turning something around in her mind. "You know, you could use this to your advantage."

"How so?"

"You could make him your bitch-boy."

Emily laughed.

"Again with the bitch-boy thing! I don't even know what a bitch-boy does."

"Everything, silly," Madison replied. "They do everything."

Aiden

One of the guys in Ms. Harwood's class had caught Emily's eye. His name was Aiden, and it made a jolt of electricity shoot up her spine when she heard his name called out with the tone of voice that invariably meant that he would soon be positioned rear end up on the side of her desk. Emily was audience to this particular form of humiliating punishment with regularity, and she was intrigued by the differences between the boys. Emily would look at their faces, which were always in profile to her, and marvel at the way each boy endured the devastatingly embarrassing punishment. She found that her gaze would continually return to his most private area to watch as the impact of the birch rod made his penis swing back and forth.

Emily watched with mouthwatering anticipation as Aiden made his way to the front of the classroom. Ms. Harwood stood behind her desk, arms crossed, her long birch rod in hand. She had a stern look on her face, with the slightest hint of a smirk. Aiden had spoken out of turn, something that Ms. Harwood did not tolerate. He stood at the side of the large oak desk. His face was beet red with embarrassment at the thought of what was coming next.

Aiden's hands were trembling as he began, with resignation, to unbuckle his belt. Emily wondered to herself how he could endure the humiliation of it. But she was keenly aroused and wanted to watch every moment. He unbuttoned his pants, and then unzipped them. The classroom was silent, such that everyone in the room could hear the sound of the zipper sliding down, beginning the reveal. Finally, Aiden placed his hands on his hips, hooking his thumbs around his belt, the waist of his pants, and his underwear, and taking a deep breath, slid them down to his ankles. He then placed his hands upon the desk. Ms. Harwood moved to stand behind him, and unceremoniously lifted the tail of his shirt up his back, exposing him further. She brought the long birch rod upward and placed it across his upturned rear end. Emily's eyes travelled down his body, and she was fascinated by the size and shape of his dick. Emily inhaled slowly, watching, anticipating, taking in every delicious moment before his punishment began.

Later in the day, with as much bravery as she could muster, Emily approached Aiden. She had folded back the sleeves of her shirt, exposing her tanned, thin forearms, and her hair, which was pulled back in a ponytail during class, had been released from its hair tie and was now cascading over her shoulders. Aiden eyed her warily as she approached.

"Hi, Aiden."

"Uh, hi, um, Emily."

She could see that he was a bit shy, and somewhat nervous, which served to make her more at ease. She figured he might be feeling self-conscious as a result of the punishment he had received that afternoon.

As gently as possible, she told him that she was sorry that he had been singled out for punishment that day. He blushed and shrugged it off, saying that Ms. Harwood was too strict and that he thought she had been unfair. Then he paused, blushed, and looked at the floor for a moment.

Without looking up, he began, "From your seat in the classroom …"

She smiled, and began blushing herself, as she knew what question he was trying to ask. She was surprised that none of the boys had asked her yet.

He made another attempt: "From your seat, you can see …" He faltered again, swallowing hard.

Finally, out of sympathy for him, she answered his unfinished question: "Everything," she said, trying not to giggle. "I can see everything."

He actually seemed relieved that he had an answer, but a moment later, he was struck by another thought.

She read his mind, and offered, "Yes, I have seen all of the boys up close," she said with a bright smile.

Emily looked Aiden up and down, the image of him bent over the desk, fully exposed to her eyes from the waist down still fresh in her mind. She was nervous but excited as she contemplated her next question.

At last, she said "While you were, um," she paused, trying to figure out how to put it, "being punished," she continued, "you seemed to … kind of enjoy it."

She laughed out of nervousness, but she noticed he was even more embarrassed.

He put his hand to his face, gave a laugh, then answered, "You, um, you noticed ... that," he said, laughed again, then finished with, "I knew that you could see me. It kind of turned me on that you were watching."

She offered him a big, warm smile as she said, "Would you like to come over to my room?" Since she knew Madison's schedule, she knew that she would have him alone.

As soon as they were in her room, Emily clicked the lock on the door, and the symbolism did not escape her that she now had him captive. She smiled a secret smile, excited by the thoughts of what she would do to him. She watched him awkwardly, sheepishly standing in the middle of the room, and she gained a sense of the power she had to compel him to do as she pleased.

He had an expectant look on his face, and he was clearly nervous. She leaned back against her desk, the sleeves of her pressed, white shirt rolled up, exposing her tanned, delicate forearms and petite hands, which she had placed on the edge of the desk to prop herself up. Her gray pleated skirt ended above her knees, and the shoes she had worn had been kicked off into the corner off the room. Her knees felt a bit weak as she observed him standing before her, knowing what was coming next.

"Did it hurt?" she inquired. "I mean, when you were punished?"

"Yes," he replied, blushing.

"Was it humiliating for you to bend over the desk and receive punishment, knowing that that everyone could see you fully?" she asked.

"Yes," he stammered, "and no. I was— I liked it that you could see."

Emily fell silent for a moment, contemplating what she might do next. This calmed her nerves considerably.

The steady, even tone of her voice surprised her as she said, "Take off your tie."

He was noticeably shaken by her sudden transition to the voice of authority, which compelled him to obey. He thought that she was remarkably attractive, and he had developed a crush on her, but she had become something else, as she had assumed a previously unknown power over him. Perhaps it was related to the old adage about imagining your audience in their underwear as a means to calm your nerves, as she had seen him in less than that. She held on to that image of him with his pants and underwear around his ankles, bent over the teacher's desk, as the source of her position of dominance.

His hands trembled a little as he reached up and untied his tie, after which he looked around for a place to put it. Emily held out her hand, and he gave to her, with what looked like a sense of relief that she had solved the problem of what to do with his tie. She giggled a little as she told him to take off his shirt. She was conscious of the fact that this was the only part of his body that she hadn't seen, and she was pleased with what she saw as his smooth, nicely built chest was exposed to her, his shirt sliding off of him and onto the chair that she was helpfully pointing out to him. Having noticed that his nervousness made her less nervous, she paused for a minute, simply observing him standing in the middle of her room with his shirt off. He made an awkward gesture of shyness, covering himself with his hands, which she immediately reprimanded him for.

"Stand straight," she told him, "and place your hands at your sides. I want to look at you for a bit longer." This seemed to electrify him, as he snapped to attention, and it appeared as though his pants were tightening a bit in the front. He had never been objectified in this manner, and it was exciting to him. In addition, he realized that he was taking orders from a girl who was younger than him.

"Take off your pants," Emily said, defiantly.

Aiden swallowed hard, looked at the floor for a moment, blushing, then slowly brought his hands to his waist to unfasten his belt. As he removed his belt, she held her hand out, as she had with his tie, and he handed the belt to her. He quickly bent down to slip off his shoes and socks, then stood up, glanced at her with a smile, took a deep breath, then unbuttoned his pants. He drew the zipper down as she observed him, her arms crossed in a casual manner, leaning against her desk, with an amused smile on her face.

She had before her the boy from her class, who was now wearing nothing but a pair of boxer briefs that were being stretched significantly between his legs. She took this moment to pause, and let the reality of what was happening sink in. He had an attentive look on his face, almost as though he was asking her to be merciful with him. Feeling a heady rush of power, she flashed him a warm smile. She took in the sight of his anticipation as he contemplated the fact that he would soon being standing before her, fully exposed, completely naked, with nothing to hide himself from her eyes. It was a calmly exciting, delicious moment she wished to savor. He remained silent, awaiting her instruction, aware that his arousal was visibly obvious to her. At last, the moment had arrived, and she could wait no longer.

There was nothing he could do to avoid it, not that he wanted to, but he was all nerves and excitement as she gestured to his remaining piece of clothing.

"Go ahead. Take off everything," she said in almost a whisper.

He took the waistband of his boxer briefs in both hands and pulled them downward.

"Slowly now," she said.

He blushed, feeling the objectification in her command to reveal himself slowly so that she might savor his reaction to being exposed to her. He tugged his boxer briefs lower, then lower still, his cock straining at the elastic.

Inch by inch, he was exposed to her. She watched, transfixed, as his smooth, pale hips, clearly defining a border between the tanned skin of his chest and the white skin that would normally be covered by his shorts, emerged into view. She inhaled sharply, watching him slowly be revealed. His cock suddenly popped out of his underwear, fully and unbelievably hard. Emily found his arousal an incredible sight to behold.

He then quickly slipped out of his boxer briefs, dropped them onto the chair with his other clothing, and turned to face her. She remained as she was, with her arms crossed, leaning up against her desk, as she quietly observed the totality of his nakedness. For several moments, they both said nothing as her mind reeled with possibilities. He was just so hard, and she had nothing to compare to this moment of supreme objectification of his naked body. She made no attempt to hide the fact that she was fully staring at his erect cock. It was thick, rather long, and though there was something menacing about the size and upward trajectory of it, there was also something charming, even cute, about the rosy pink smoothness of it, and the caramel-colored skin stretched tightly along the shaft. She looked at his balls and marveled at the feeling of seeing something so inherently male, yet so sensitive and defenseless.

"Show me how you masturbate," she said at last. She could see how her words affected him. She could see everything. He was nervous to be so naked to begin with, and now she was going to see him so much more exposed.

Innocently, she added, "I want to see how you do it. And I want to know how often you do it. And what you think about. Show me how you do it and tell me everything."

He laughed, involuntarily, from embarrassment, but she could tell how turned on he was by the suggestion. He was slow to comply, but seeing that she was serious, standing there in her crisp white shirt and pleated gray skirt, her feet planted firmly, as though defying him to disobey a direct order. She returned her arms to a crossed position and looked at him expectantly.

He brought his right hand upward, wrapped it slowly around his cock, and began sliding his hand back and forth over the head of it. Her lips curled into a wicked little smile as she watched him with great interest.

"You're the only boy from class I have seen completely naked. And fully hard."

She liked the effect that her words had on him. Everything she said seemed to make him feel more aware of how exposed he was to her. He flushed red with embarrassment, having never masturbated in front of anyone, let alone a cute girl who was demanding it of him. She uncrossed her arms and placed them on the edge of the desk as she lowered her gaze to watch him pleasure himself. She was silent for some moments before looking up and prompting him.

"And you were going to tell me how often you masturbate?"

"Well, the truth is, I don't have a lot of privacy here, so ..."

"Oh, right," Emily said, laughing at the thought of how completely exposed the boys generally were.

They were standing just a few feet apart, and the sun raked across his naked body while he played with his cock and admitted the most intimate information to her.

"Well, you have your privacy here, in my room," she mused. "I hope that you don't mind me watching," she said in sincerity.

He blushed, then answered her question: "I don't mind you watching."

It was Emily's turn to flush red. His eyes naturally dropped to the floor under her gaze, and for several minutes, they said nothing. She leaned against the edge of her desk and took her time in assessing his body. She pressed her palms against the edge of her desk. She bit her lip.

Finally, she broke the silence, saying, "Come here."

He crossed the few feet between them, and she leaned up as he approached and kissed him. For several minutes they remained in this embrace, and the scent and heat of his body electrified her, as did the fact that he was completely nude while she remained fully clothed. This aspect was not lost on either of them. She felt undeniably in charge, while he felt entirely in her hands. Which he was, as her hands made contact with his chest, sliding up his body slowly, feeling every inch of him. She brought one hand around his neck, pulling him closer, as the other hand made its way downward, coming to rest on his hip.

The afternoon sun was a soft orange glow through the window blinds, and the silence of the moment was sexually charged. She was so wet that she would soon have to remove her panties, but first, she had him take a step back so that she could look at him again. Her eyes traveled slowly down his body, coming to rest between his legs. She glanced up at him with a look of curiosity.

"I want to watch you make yourself come," she whispered.

She suggested that he lie down on her bed. She followed his movements as he crossed the room and was thrilled by the sight of his large, masculine body lowering itself onto her bed. She sat down on the edge of the bed, her eyes tracing the lines of his body as he reached for his cock and began masturbating again. He looked up at her with a lustful haze in his eyes, and she returned the look as she made herself comfortable, relaxing onto the edge of the bed, allowing her gaze to travel up and down the length of his body. She studied his movements, and the expression on his face as he performed this private act for her. She loved the feeling of control that she had. She had never seen a boy completely naked, and certainly not sexually pleasuring himself right in front of her. After a while, she couldn't deny her curiosity.

"Would it be OK if I played with it?" she asked.

She hopped up on the bed, throwing her bare leg over his body and straddling his upper thighs. She steadied herself by placing her hands on his hips, and thrilled to the warmth and smooth, muscled surface of his body. She looked down and noticed the hem of her skirt draped across his erect cock. When she pulled her skirt back, securing her modesty by pressing it down between her spread legs, it caused a reveal, of sorts, of his most intimate body parts. She laughed, excited that she was about to feel his dick in her hands. *It looks so much bigger close up,* she thought to herself. She looked him in the eye as she contemplated what she was about to do.

"Put your hands above your head," she demanded warily. He did, and groaned with the pleasure of having her sitting astride his body while he was so fully hard. He wanted her to touch him so badly, his eyes betraying the lustful desire that he felt. She looked at him with half desire and half curiosity, and allowed her gaze to slowly travel down his body until she was directly staring at his cock, which was thrust upward, begging to be touched. She left one hand on his hip, while the other slowly traced a line to his cock. She had never seen one so close to her, and she was enthralled by the opportunity to take it in her hand. She felt an electric charge as she delicately slid one fingertip up the length of it, and noticed the effect it had on him. She was surprised to see it jump. It sprang away from her touch, then bounced back. She paused, looked at him, and saw the erotic desperation on his face. She smiled, and returned her attention to the pretty, new plaything between his legs. She slowly, carefully wrapped her petite hand around it. The feeling was unique, in that the skin was soft, like silk, yet the cock itself was hard, like it was made of marble. She held him in her hand and watched the desire course through him. Slowly, she slid her hand up and down his length. She was fascinated. She felt a primal sexual attraction, yet she felt repulsion at the same time. He was the same cute boy she had a crush on in class, but he also had this man part, this big dick that she now had in her hand. She hadn't even thought about the fact that it was made to fit inside of her, as it looked entirely too large for that. Its skin was smooth and pink, and it was curiously shaped, like an exotic underwater animal. It was cute, in a way, but the thickness and the weight of it was intimidating. The scent of him was in the air. It was unique and personal, and it inspired an overwhelming sexual desire to course through her, a throbbing sensation that took over her entire body and became focused between her legs. He closed his eyes, overcome with pleasure and a feeling of embarrassment that he was completely naked while she was fully dressed. It suddenly struck her what an extremely powerful position she was in—her bare legs, pressed against his naked skin on either side of his thighs, her delicate, feminine hand, holding his enormously erect cock.

    He was very close to coming. She observed him in this state, seeing the overwhelmingly pleasurable sensation that the slow, gentle movement of her hand was causing, and she felt a fascinating feeling of being completely dominant over him. She wondered what would happen if she simply stopped. So she did. She took her hand away from his cock and placed it on his hip as she stared into his eyes. She was rewarded with a look of desperation, a pleading look that revealed the absolute power she had over him. It was a delicious, extraordinary feeling as she sat astride his exposed body, observing his desperate desire, having him entirely at her mercy and held captive in her room. Her mind raced with images of what she might do to him.

"I will make you a deal," Emily said. Her lips curled into a little smile as she continued, "I will make you come, but first you have to promise me something."

Lying on the bed, his arms raised above his head, with Emily sitting astride his naked body, he inadvertently licked his lips.

"Anything. I'll do anything."

She felt a rush of desire in hearing him say that and taking in the sight of him lying beneath her. She took his cock in her hand again, and while slowly stroking it up and down, made him promise that from now on, he was to only masturbate in front of her, in her room. His eyes betrayed the lust and excitement he felt to hear her say that, and he quickly agreed. He was on the edge, and with a few more strokes of her hand, she witnessed a sight that she had never seen before. His entire body trembled and convulsed as a thick, white liquid came shooting out of the tiny opening at the end of his cock. It made an arc in the air, and then fell upon his chest, followed by a second, and then a third. She watched in amazement, witnessing the wondrous sight of a boy having an orgasm.

Later, after she had kissed him "goodbye for now," she slipped off her dripping wet panties and threw herself onto the bed. The scent of him surrounded her as she lifted her skirt and used her fingers to play with herself, making herself come within minutes, then twice more, thoughts of all that she might do with him racing through her imagination.

Madison and James

James arrived at the main courtyard at 6 p.m. on Friday, precisely as Madison had directed. He waited for her, and she arrived shortly.

"How romantic," Madison noted, smiling warmly. "This is the place where we met," she said, indicating the punishment circle, which was uncharacteristically empty.

"Yes, Miss, I remember," James recalled, an embarrassed smile on his face. "If I may say, Miss, I was incredibly attracted to you instantly, and I haven't stopped thinking about you. I was so surprised when you showed up in my dorm room."

"Yeah, well, call me M, and escort me to the cafeteria, James."

"Actually, if you like, M, I thought you might enjoy something I have planned."

James indicated the backpack he was carrying.

"Um, hiking?" she asked.

"No, not hiking," he said with a laugh. "I didn't have a picnic basket, so …"

"A picnic? My goodness, that is romantic. And what do you think I want to eat on this picnic?"

"Uh, I have a bit of everything, but I also talked to your roommate, Miss Emily, and she gave me some suggestions."

Madison just stared at James for a moment, unsure of what to do about the fact that she was really touched by how thoughtful he had been.

"Well, then, do you also have a location selected for our picnic, loverboy? Because I know where we are going right afterward."

James offered her his arm, and she took it, trying to put out of her mind for the moment all of the things she was going to do to him that evening.

After their dinner date concluded, Madison brought James back to her room. She pushed him down onto the floor and began kissing him as she pulled his shirt off. His eyelids were heavy with desire and she could see that he was hard in his regulation trousers, so she took them off, and soon had him naked. Then she took his hands, positioned them against a leg of the bed, and tied them in place with a length of soft nylon rope. She sat back on her heels and looked into his eyes to gauge his reaction to his newly acquired imprisonment. He was so very naked before her—his hands, bound and his bare butt, on her floor. His dick was erect, arcing upward between his legs, which were spread apart, as she knelt between them. She smiled deviously at her captive, and he swallowed hard, appearing a bit nervous but nevertheless incredibly turned on to find himself tied up and completely under her control. She placed a hand upon his chest and slowly slid her fingertips down the front of his body, purposefully avoiding touching his cock.

Then she sat back, retrieved a long black silk scarf from her dresser drawer, and tied it across his face as a blindfold. She sat back on her heels again, seeing him anew. He was guy she was interested in, and she had wondered what it would be like to kiss him, but now she saw him in an entirely new light. The sight of him sitting stark naked on the floor, his hands tied to the bed leg, and his eyes blindfolded made him appear so embarrassingly obedient that she couldn't help but laugh.

She could see, in spite of the blindfold, that her laughter made him nervous. She leaned forward and kissed him, placing her hands upon his body possessively. She began to explore her captive's body with her hands, making a thorough assessment of his physicality. She was surprised and delighted by how responsive he was to her touch. She could sense that he had entirely given himself over to her, and that he fully understood that she could do anything she desired with his body. She retrieved a cloth tape measure from her desk drawer. She returned and wrapped one hand around the base of his dick, while the other hand held the measuring tape pressed against the length of him.

"What are you doing, Miss?" James asked.

"I'm measuring your cock," she replied matter-of-factly.

She took note of the measurement, then wrapped the measuring tape around the middle of his shaft.

"What are you doing now?" he asked.

"Still measuring your cock, James."

She took a small moleskin journal that she kept in a drawer beside her bed and opened it to a page that had a list of boys' names, each followed by a set of measurements. There was a list of names to which she added James's name along with the newly acquired measurements.

"What are you doing now?" James asked.

"Writing down the measurements of your cock," she replied, then she kissed him.

Then, unable to resist, she leaned forward, took his balls in her hand, listened to the moan that escaped his lips as she gripped him firmly, and pressed her lips against the head of his cock. She opened her mouth and descended upon him, and he moaned with unrestrained lust and desire. She spent just a minute or two licking the tip of his cock, then she sat back.

"Tell me you love this. Tell me that you love being my plaything."

He responded in a hoarse whisper that he did, prompting her to slap him across the dick. He gasped at the pain of having his dick spanked, and she placed her hand on the back of his head and kissed him deeply. She teased him, tormented him as she slapped his dick repeatedly, and then kissed him again.

After some time playing with him in this manner, she raised the hem of her dress, revealing the fact that she didn't wear panties, and straddled his face.

"Lick me, James," she said in a low, urgent whisper, then thrust her hips, pressing her soft, pink lips against his.

She began riding his tongue, aware of the fact that being blindfolded was driving him mad with the desire to see her naked pussy against his face. When, at last, she came, she slid her hips up and off of him, and took his cock in her hand. She jerked him off, hard and fast, and within moments, he came all over himself. Eventually, she would untie him, but she wasn't quite done with him yet. She untied the blindfold from across his eyes and kissed him. Then she ran her fingers through the pools of cum on his chest and allowed it to drip off of her fingertips into his mouth.

"Your tongue is so talented, James. I think I might just have to keep you tied to my bedpost."

"Yes, Miss," he replied, and she was intrigued by the fact that he sounded earnest in his response.

The Six

Over the course of the first few weeks, they had become known simply as "The Six," a group made up of Charlotte, Sarah, Juliette, Maya, Madison, and Emily, and they had become really close, good friends. They met in Charlotte and Sarah's suite to hear Charlotte's idea about some project she was excited about.

Charlotte sat in silence for a moment, then said, "Well here's the plan. We make a database—like a guidebook, if you will, and we call it 'The Book.' Like, you know, another famous social platform, but this one is different. First off, nudity is not censored; it is required. Second, it's just the boys in the school."

"The entire school?!" Juliette asked.

"No, not the entire school," replied Charlotte. "Just the cute ones," she said with a wink.

"So, photos, and stats," Sarah volunteered.

"Exactly," Charlotte replied, "with photos of each of the boys, accompanied by all pertinent information about them. We interview them, by which I mean *interrogate* them, and find out everything we want to know. They will understand that they have to fall in line, and we end up with a really useful tool for us to use."

"Brilliant," Juliette responded, as she began to imagine the scenario. "So do we bring them here, one at a time?"

"Yes. We just have to put them at ease," Charlotte said. "We will cheerfully explain that their full cooperation is mandatory."

The other girls laughed, as they realized the position each of the boys would be in. The only real choice available to them would be to enthusiastically consent, and do exactly as they were told, regardless of what that might be.

The following weekend, it began. The boy they had decided would go first was a boy named Kyle, who was now standing in the center of Charlotte and Sarah's suite. The room was lined with armchairs and sofas, upon which the six girls sat comfortably, forming a judge's panel. They noted that Kyle appeared uncharacteristically nervous in contrast to the cool and calm demeanor he generally projected. As Charlotte had pointed out when they had invented the plan, it would be rather intimidating for each of the boys when they realized that they were alone with the six of them, as the girls held an unquestioned authority over them.

"Just relax," Charlotte said to Kyle. "We won't make you do anything you don't want to." She paused, then added, "So with everything you consent to, we will assume that your compliance is due to the fact that you are willing to do so."

"Yes, Miss," Kyle said as he nodded, showing that he understood. Then he swallowed hard, realizing that, though he could refuse to cooperate, this refusal would come at a very high price. And so, he stood before them, nervously anticipating what was going to happen. He didn't have to wait long.

"Take off your clothes, please," Charlotte said, as the six girls had decided that this would immediately put each of the boys in the proper mindset for the duration of the interview.

They could see that he was taken aback, not because he hadn't thought something like this might happen, but he certainly didn't expect that it would begin this way. So he began to undress, and the girls went silent. Their silence was even more intimidating than having to take off his clothes, as it heightened his awareness that they were watching him intently. This is not to say that they were leaning forward, staring. The girls' attention was even more pronounced by the fact that they appeared completely relaxed, sitting back in their seats, eyeing the young male body as it emerged from its clothing.

Finally, Kyle slid his underwear down and stood before them, completely naked. Emily, whose task it was to take photos, did just that. Not all at once, of course. Rather, it was one single snap and whirr of the shutter that interrupted the silence in the room.

And then Charlotte said, "Tell us about yourself, Kyle."

He stood still, with his hands at his sides, his eyes lowered. Standing naked before the group of girls as they casually observed him was far more intimidating than he could have imagined.

"Um, well, what do you want to know, Miss?" he replied.

Sarah smiled at the response. *That's right*, she thought to herself. *You'll tell us anything we want to know.*

"How tall are you?" she asked. *Best to start with the easy questions,* she reasoned.

"Six feet tall, Miss," he replied. "A little over six feet."

"How much do you weigh?"

"One hundred seventy-five pounds, Miss."

"How long is your cock?" Charlotte asked impatiently.

"Do you mean, when it's hard, Miss?" Kyle asked.

"Yes, when it's hard," Madison said, laughing. "We can all see how long it is soft."

Though this was true, they could also see that his cock was slowly becoming erect.

"Five inches, Miss," he replied. "A little over five inches." He noticed that Sarah was writing down each of the answers he was giving. What he did not know was that all of his answers would accompany the photos that Emily was taking, and be made available, online, to all of the girls at the school.

"What is the circumference?" Madison asked.

"Four inches, Miss. Almost."

"Turn around, please" he heard Emily say.

He turned around, and he heard the snap of the camera's shutter.

Emily had to make sure she had photos of the boys from all angles.

"Turn back around," he heard Charlotte say.

He turned, blushing due to the fact that he had become fully erect. No one made mention of his erection, but he heard the sound of Emily's camera once again.

"What are your interests?" Charlotte asked. "Like hobbies, or extracurricular activities, or what classes do you like, you know."

"Mainly science and art, Miss," he responded. "I'm in band. I play percussion, Miss."

Emily tried not to laugh, envisioning him playing the drums while naked.

"I like weightlifting and I like writing. I like drawing, and um, photography."

"Do you masturbate often?" Maya asked.

"No, Miss," Kyle responded. "Masturbation is not allowed for the male students, Miss."

This was true, as per the handbook, but the there was no rule preventing the females from having the boys masturbate in front of them.

"Play with your penis for the next sixty seconds," Maya said while looking at her watch.

"Yes, Miss," Kyle replied, and began masturbating, hoping that one of the girls would tell him when to stop, since he was not wearing a watch himself. He also desperately hoped he wouldn't accidentally make himself come, as this would undoubtedly get him in a lot of trouble with the girls.

The girls watched silently as Kyle stroked his dick, until Maya told him to stop.

"Now pull your penis up and hold it against your abdomen so that we can look at your balls," Maya directed.

Kyle did so, and Emily took a photo. Receiving no further instructions, Kyle remained in this position.

"What embarrasses you, Kyle?" Charlotte asked.

Sarah had to laugh, since clearly, what the girls were doing to him now had to be extremely embarrassing for him. For his part, Kyle thought that the best thing for him to do was to be completely honest.

"I am a bit embarrassed that my dick is not as big as I would like it to be," he admitted.

"Yeah, you do have a small penis," Maya replied, "so I can see how that would embarrass you. And what else?"

When the girls had asked Kyle every probing, personal question they could think of, they allowed him to put his clothes back on and leave, just in time for the next boy on the list. They accomplished interrogating about twenty boys on the first day and continued after that to document as many as they could handle, with an eye on including as many as they were able.

Over the next several weeks, The Six invited each of the boys they were interested in to come over and undergo an examination, though the format continued to change as the girls got creative about how they wanted to address each of the young men, and how to best exploit them individually.

Antony

The Academy had been built on a large parcel of land. The school buildings themselves were located toward the front of the property, though set back from the road a bit and secured by a tall fence. Behind the school buildings were a few hundred acres of woods owned by the Academy. They weren't designated for any purpose other than hiking or the general enjoyment of the land's natural beauty.

Charlotte led Antony out into the woods, past the old barn, and across the bridge over the small, meandering creek. They continued until they reached a dilapidated stone foundation of what had been a cottage at one time. Charlotte smiled at him in an attempt to calm his nerves. However, Antony couldn't help but think there was something a bit sinister behind her smile. It actually served to increase his anxiety about what was about to happen.

When they arrived at the old cottage, Charlotte gestured for him to enter. There was no longer a door, just a stone archway, and as he walked in, he saw that there was no longer a roof either. Seated on the ledge of what had once been a brick fireplace were Juliette, Sarah, and Maya. Madison and Emily were absent, and the other girls had noticed that they had become more and more unavailable, as they were each spending time with their respective boys.

"Hello, Antony," the girls said, practically in unison. There was something ominous in the way they said it.

Antony stepped forward into the middle of what once had been a room and mumbled a "hello" in return. Sunlight streamed through the opening where the roof used to be. The girls were seated on the ledge of the stone fireplace, in the cool shadows of the edge of the room. He nervously looked from one girl to the next, unsure of what to do with himself.

Suddenly, Charlotte spoke up.

"We invited you here today because we think that you should be included in our database."

Antony stood still, listening, wondering where this was going. He felt a pit of nervous fear in his stomach.

"What that means," she continued, "is that you will be required to do exactly, and I do mean *exactly,* what is requested of you. Do you think that you can do that?"

Antony looked at the ground, suddenly feeling very intimidated by the girls. There was something in the tone of Charlotte's voice and the way that the four girls were looking at him which gave him pause.

"Yes, Miss," Antony replied, his voice almost cracking with the nervous excitement he was feeling.

"Good," Charlotte said. "Take off your clothes."

Antony was terrified, not knowing what all might be expected of him, but even more terrified of disobeying a direct order from a female student. He had thought that, surely, they weren't going to make him strip naked in front of them, but he now realized they were going to do precisely that.

"We want you to understand that this process is not going to be easy for you," Charlotte explained. "But we think that you will find the reward to be worth it. So we highly recommend that you comply with every order you hear. Do you understand?"

"Yes, Miss" Antony responded, feeling awkward as he removed his clothing and stood at attention before them.

What followed was several minutes of silence.

Juliette, Sarah, and Maya looked to Charlotte, who smiled menacingly. They couldn't help but chuckle at his reaction as he blushed from embarrassment, trembling slightly with fear.

Antony had never felt so naked in his life as he did at that moment. Each of the four girls took their time in assessing his body. The previous weekend they had interrogated Kyle, then Justin, then Daniel and Tyler, so they couldn't help but compare Antony to the previous boys. And so they stared, taking in the sight and enjoying the delicious decadence of the moment.

Sarah, who was filling in for Emily as the photographer, snapped a photo.

"So, you're uncircumcised?" Juliette asked.

"Yes, Miss," Antony replied.

"Yeah, Sarah pointed that out to me in the shower room last week," Charlotte commented.

"I'm kind of fascinated," Juliette said with a sly smile.

"OK, you're weird," Charlotte said with a shrug.

"You don't find it fascinating? How totally different it looks?" Juliette peered at Charlotte quizzically.

"I'd totally have him circumcised if it were up to me," Charlotte replied.

"Wow, did you hear that, Antony?" Juliette asked. "Charlotte here wants to circumcise you."

All four girls had to laugh at the look of trepidation on his face. Then Charlotte changed the subject.

"We need to make an assessment of your physical fitness, Antony," Charlotte declared, "so you will need to perform thirty jumping jacks, thirty push-ups, and thirty sit-ups. Begin."

Antony blushed again from embarrassment, but he was also somewhat relieved that he had something to do, as he had become very nervous simply standing before them, fully naked. As he began the thirty jumping jacks, he could hear the girls giggle as his dick bounced up and down with his movements. He felt particularly embarrassed that his body was displayed in such a ridiculous manner and that his dick was bouncing and slapping against his abdomen and thighs as he performed the exercises.

When he had completed the prescribed calisthenics, he returned to a standing position and awaited the next order. It was beginning to dawn on him that the girls were serious about making this "interrogation" deeply embarrassing for him.

The girls were practically delirious from laughing. Antony's face was flushed from the exertion, which added to his look of embarrassment.

"Do you masturbate?" asked Maya.

"No, Miss," Antony admitted. "Male students are prohibited from—"

"Right," Sarah interrupted. "Why do you always ask that, Maya? They always give the same response!"

"I *like it* that they always have to give the same response. I like it when they admit that they aren't allowed to masturbate."

"OK, well show us how you would do it with your uncut penis," Juliette said.

Although he was incredibly embarrassed to do so, at the same time, he was hopelessly turned on by being allowed to, and so he nervously placed his hand around his cock and slowly began to masturbate as the four girls watched in fascination. Within moments, he had an erection. The girls observed, silently, as he played with himself for their amusement.

"What do you think about when you, well, fantasize, since you aren't allowed to masturbate?" Maya asked after a minute or two.

"Um, different ... things," Antony stammered. "Girls ..." he added, trailing off.

"Any girl in particular?" Sarah inquired.

"Yes," he replied, hesitating.

"Who?" asked Juliette. "You have to tell us!"

Antony paused, clearly embarrassed that he was being compelled to reveal his secret.

"You," he said at last.

Charlotte, Maya, and Sarah burst out laughing.

Juliette felt a peculiar sensation. She was slightly embarrassed, but she also felt flattered that he would fantasize about her.

"Did you hear that, Jules?" Maya asked, amused. "He fantasizes about you."

Juliette smiled in return, and fixed Antony with a predatory smile.

Sarah added, "I don't know, I mean, that doesn't seem fair that he has been fantasizing about you without your knowledge. I think that a punishment is in order, don't you think?"

"Oh, most definitely," Juliette seconded.

A couple of days earlier, Juliette had suggested that they have some way to measure the boys, to ensure accuracy, but when she brought out the ruler she owned, the other girls looked at the thick, heavy piece of hardwood and decided it would be better put to use as an implement of punishment.

"Where did you get this?" Charlotte asked.

"I brought it from home. I've had it forever, and it's old. Like, when-they-made-stuff-out-of-really-heavy-wood old," Juliette replied.

"Well, we should definitely have this available to get an accurate measurement—because boys lie—but we should also have it available to spank their naked butts," Charlotte suggested.

All of the girls agreed. Then Charlotte made it even better by suggesting that they have the boys tied up with their hands above their heads. To that end, they paid a visit to the cottage the following day and threw a long length of rope over an exposed rafter in the adjoining room of the dilapidated cottage. They left one end hanging straight down. The other end, they would tie to a large iron ring bolt that had been mounted to the fireplace when the house was built, for what purpose they couldn't imagine—but it came in handy for tying up boys, as it turned out.

"Stop masturbating now, Antony," Charlotte announced. The four girls watched their naked captive comply, letting his hands fall to his sides. His erection remained, as he stood before them awaiting his next order.

"The initiate will get on his hands and knees."

He did, and Charlotte continued, "Now crawl, on your hands and knees, and follow me."

Since each of the girls knew what was coming next, they arose at once and made their way to the adjoining room.

"Come this way," Charlotte said in a cheerful voice. The girls situated themselves in the next room as Charlotte guided Antony to the center of the room.

"Now stand up," she said as he was directly below where the rope was hanging from the rafter. She wrapped the rope three times round both of his wrists, then wrapped it three times between his wrists, and then tied it off with a bow. The other end of the rope was pulled downward, which raised his arms above his head, until his naked body was stretched tight, and he was practically standing on his toes. Then the rope was secured to the ring bolt on the fireplace.

When Charlotte was satisfied with the way that Antony was presented, both in the aesthetic of the display and the practical sense of making him vulnerable to whatever they might do to him, she took a seat next to the other two girls. They expressed their admiration of her work and commented on the way that the tightness of the rope kept his body so firmly in position. Sarah had the wooden ruler at the ready, and she offered it to the other two girls, allowing them to determine who might go first.

"Who wants to take a whack at it first?" she asked, laughing at her own joke. Both she and the other girls thought that Juliette should go first, but she deferred, perhaps because she wanted to watch. Ultimately, Charlotte took the ruler first and held it pressed against the Antony's well-formed and vulnerable ass. She brought it back a good distance, then swung it fast and hard, and it produced a loud smack as it struck its target. Antony gasped—out of surprise, but also out of pain—as the ruler left a long pink mark across his butt. Then Maya got up and gave him a hard whack. Then Sarah took a turn, and again, a satisfying mark across his bare cheeks was the result. As she offered the ruler to Juliette, Charlotte spoke up, and suggested that perhaps they should leave Juliette to spend some time with Antony, in light of the confession that he had made. Sarah agreed, and the girls giggled as they persuaded Juliette to not go too easy on him.

She assured them that she wouldn't, but when she was alone with him and the sound of their voices had faded in the distance, she admitted, "I don't really need to spank you if you would rather that I didn't. I know that we have been a bit hard on you today."

She was sincere in her gesture, as she did feel a bit sorry for him, yet she still took the opportunity to look him up and down in his fully compromised state of captivity. She even thought his naked dick looked kind of cute, all hard and exposed, and the way that the rope bondage displayed his body was deliciously obscene. She didn't know if she would ever look at him the same way again after this, though she decided that was a good thing. It would define the relationship between them that she had observed him this way, and it would continually remind them both that she had the upper hand in any negotiation.

"Thank you, Miss," Antony said in a way she found quite disarming. Then he said something that surprised her.

"I think I would rather that you did. I agree with all that was said today, that ... well, I have fantasized about you, and I didn't really have your permission. I think that I would feel better about it if you punished me, Miss."

Juliette took a step back and considered what Antony had said. She felt the weight of the wooden ruler in her hands as she examined every inch of him. The air was cool, and the woods were silent. All she could hear were birds chirping and him breathing, as well as the occasional creak of the wooden rafter as his body shifted ever so slightly. She contemplated his erect cock, displayed for anyone to see, along with the rest of his nakedness. Then, having made her decision—which she realized with some pleasure was hers alone to make—she slowly brought the ruler up between his legs until it was pressed against his balls.

"OK," she finally offered in response, "spread your legs a bit wider for me, Antony."

He inhaled sharply as the realization dawned on him that contrary to his expectation, she did not intend to spank his butt as he had assumed. A soft whimper escaped his lips as he complied, spreading his legs wider, making him more vulnerable to her than he could have imagined. She savored the moment as she allowed his anticipation to build. She could see that he was simultaneously afraid of her and incredibly turned by her. She felt an amazing sensation of control, as every little movement of the ruler had him on edge. He was like a puppet suspended from the rafters. She could make him dance for her, and at the same time, bear witness to his arousal in doing so. He had admitted to pleasuring himself to thoughts of her. *What has he thought about?* she wondered to herself. *And what can I make him do for me?* She was getting the idea that she wouldn't have to "make" him do anything—that he would do anything she wanted at the merest suggestion. She looked forward to finding out. Time seemed to stretch out before them, languid and peaceful, time in which to explore the depths of his infatuation with and devotion to her. The ruler didn't feel particularly heavy in her hand, yet it was a substantial piece of wood. It had been polished smooth, and it slid effortlessly between his legs.

She gave him a hard slap and watched his reaction. He gasped, his whole body reacting, and he almost yelped from the pain. She observed him, amused, and quickly gave him another, harder slap. His reaction was even better this time, and so she learned quickly that the harder she spanked him, the more satisfying his reaction was for her.

"So tell me, when you fantasize about me, what exactly do you think about?"

Before he had time to answer, she gave him another hard slap, then went back to caressing him gently.

"I think about kissing you, Miss," he responded when he had recovered. "All over."

"All over my body? So, do you picture me undressed?"

"Yes, Miss. I fantasize about undressing you."

She spanked him nice and hard across his balls, and he cried out in pain, yet still kept his legs spread for her.

"So where exactly do you fantasize about kissing me?"

"All over your body, Miss. And between your legs."

"So you fantasize about licking my pussy?"

"Yes, Miss."

"Where do you want to lick me? I want to hear you say it."

"I want to lick your pussy, Miss," he replied, practically in a whisper. Juliette whacked him hard, which made his body convulse, and his head jerked back as he emitted an anguished moan. Before he had time to recover, she whacked him again, the smooth, flat surface making a satisfyingly audible slap as it struck his naked balls.

"I want to hear you say that again."

"I want to lick your pussy, Miss," he replied, sounding out of breath. His body tensed, anticipating another slap across his balls, but instead, she stepped forward and kissed him. They kissed for some moments, then she took a step backward.

"Thank you, Miss," he said again, softly.

"Thank you for what?"

"Thank you for punishing me, Miss."

"Oh, do you think I am done with you?" She laughed, genuinely amused, then brought the ruler up between his legs again.

"Because I'm not done with you. Not yet."

She spanked him hard across the balls, then repeated that a few more times, enjoying his reaction, then she began to lightly tap the tip of his erect cock.

"OK," she said with resolve, sounding as though she had just made a decision. She moved to his side and gave him one hard slap of the ruler across his butt, then dropped it to her side and went to untie him. When his hands were waist-high, she untied the rope around his wrists. Though he was now free, he remained in place.

"Get on your knees," she commanded. "Now masturbate for me."

He blushed, somehow still embarrassed, but placed his hand around his cock and began to pleasure himself before her as she'd ordered, a delicious sight for her.

"I have seen you naked, and you have confessed your fantasies to me, and now I want to watch you make yourself come while you think about me." She sat down on the edge of an old, wooden armchair as she spoke.

"Furthermore, I am going to give you some new rules. One, you are no longer allowed to play with your dick without my permission. Do you understand?"

"Yes, Miss," he replied.

"What that means, is that if you feel compelled to masturbate, you need to come to me and ask for my permission. And then I will decide if you are allowed to or not. So let's give that a test. Stop touching your cock and place your hands at your sides."

He did as she directed, and she almost laughed at how hard his dick appeared, desperate to be touched again.

After a moment or two, she said, "Good boy. You may begin again."

The look of relief on his face was evident. She noticed that his hand was moving very slowly along the shaft of his cock, which she imagined was so that he wouldn't come too quickly. However, she didn't want to make it easy for him, so she told him to move his hand faster. She could hear him groan as he followed her order, trying to restrain himself.

"I can see that you are trying not to come too quickly, which I appreciate, as it brings me to the next rule. You are not allowed to come without my permission. When you get close, you may ask, and I will decide. Do you understand?"

"Yes, Miss" he replied, his voice strained. "May I ... may I come now, Miss?"

"Yes," she answered, sounding amused.

No sooner had she spoken, his body began to tremble. Then his back arched, his head fell back with his mouth open, and a wildly desperate moan was unleashed. He seemed to lock into position, with his hips thrust forward, as his orgasm caused come to shoot upward, in a long arc, three times in quick succession. She was simultaneously appalled and aroused by the extraordinary display.

As his orgasm subsided, she crossed over to him and told him to stand up. Their eyes met, and she could see a look of wonderment on his face. He had a newfound respect for and devotion to her. She kissed him, and for a moment, everything melted away except for their kiss. And then, every thought came rushing back: the fact that he was naked, that he had just masturbated for her, and that she had punished his balls with the ruler. She placed her hands on his hips, feeling his bare skin, and he wrapped his arms around her. For several minutes, they remained like this. She was surprised that his dick became hard again, and so she took the opportunity to feel it in her hand. She moved her hand slowly up and down the shaft, listened to his breathing become heavier, and saw that his eyes had a dazed look to them, which she realized was due to his heightened state of arousal.

"It's so easy to control a boy," Juliette said aloud as she stared at the cock in her hand. Almost effortlessly, she had caused him to experience fantastic pain, and now, excruciating pleasure. And he had been naked throughout, and clearly her property. She wondered what all she might do with him. Or do *to* him. Her mind reeled with the possibilities. And then, at once, her mind cleared, and she was entirely in the moment. Every movement of her hand on his cock was bringing him closer to coming again. She had adjusted herself such that she was standing beside him, which allowed her other hand access to travel up and down his back, feeling the beautiful curve of his butt, and the strength in his broad shoulders. She observed the look on his face, gauging the effect the movement of her hands was having upon him. She occasionally allowed her gaze to drift downward, and she was still a bit shocked by the size of the dick in her hand. It appeared larger, somehow, when she was holding it. She noticed that her thumb and fingers barely touched one another when they were wrapped tightly around him. And it felt incredibly soft and smooth, but deliciously hard at the same time. The tip of his cock was a pretty pink, and almost cute in appearance, and she thrilled to the way that he trembled slightly when her fingers brushed against it. She had a brief thought that involved whipping the very tip of his cock somehow, wondering how he would respond to pain in such a sensitive area. She decided that she was going to have to experiment with his naked body, to find out what all she could do with him.

"Ahhh," his moan broke the relative silence, "may I come now, Miss?"

"Yes, you may."

She watched him come again, which was more rewarding now that she had made him come with her own hand, and she could feel the throbbing pulse of his cock as he ejaculated. As he recovered, she retained a hold on his dick as she kissed him. She felt it become soft and finally released it as they remained in an embrace that lasted several minutes.

"I guess we should get going now," she said at last. "It's getting late."

"Um, thank you, Miss. Thank you for everything."

She laughed, and said, "Of course, Antony."

She flashed him a dazzling smile, and he blushed in return.

"Um, where are my clothes?" he asked, looking around with wonder at the old cottage.

Juliette burst out laughing, having forgotten, with all that had transpired, what the plan had been.

"Uh, yeah, well, you see," she began, and caught sight of Antony's look of fear.

"Don't worry. The girls left your clothes at the edge of the woods. It's not far," she said, laughing.

She gave him a wink and couldn't help but laugh at the look on his face.

"C'mon, naked boy, let's take a walk through the woods."

Emily and Aiden

Emily had Aiden in her room after classes almost every other day, and she watched him take off his clothes and masturbate for her each time. At the end of the second week, however, she felt daring. She wanted to go further. She wanted to feel him touching her.

When Aiden knocked softly on her door that Friday, she opened it and greeted him with a dazzling smile. She locked the door behind him once he was inside her room and wasted no time in delivering her first order.

"Strip naked," she said with a bright, musical laugh at the thrill of her control over him.

She watched as he obediently dropped his clothes onto the empty chair beside him and return to a standing position, now completely nude. She made him wait, knowing that he would be at his most vulnerable while waiting for the next instruction. She drew the moment out, breathing in slowly, leisurely taking in the sight of him as she allowed her gaze to travel up and down the length of his body. Though she had seen him in this position several times now, it was still incredibly exciting to watch him comply with her order to strip.

It was an excruciatingly erotic sensation for Aiden to stand before Emily as she silently assessed his naked form. He watched as she nonchalantly reached up and pulled off her hair tie, allowing her hair to cascade across her shoulders. She was staring directly at his cock as she did this.

Suddenly, a thought occurred to her, and she held the hair tie out to him.

"Put this on your dick," she said, making sure to have a serious look on her face so that he wouldn't hesitate to comply.

He looked at the tight little hair tie, then, with a slight grin, took it in his hand and stretched it around his cock, sliding it down until it encircled the base of his erection. He felt an erotic sensation that caused him to blush. While it was slightly embarrassing, it turned him on to wear his classmate's hair tie fastened tightly around his dick.

He looked up at Emily expectantly, and she smiled with approval as she instructed him to begin masturbating. He took hold of his cock in one hand and slowly slid his hand back and forth, his eyes closing as he felt the extraordinary pleasure of playing with himself in front of a girl.

Emily felt her body heat rising as she watched the sensation of pleasure overwhelm him. She didn't take her eyes off of him, thrilled by the feeling of control.

"Do it with both hands," she said, and watched as he wrapped his other hand around himself and began to thrust with his hips ever so slightly. The afternoon sun was their ever-present partner in these trysts, its soft orange glow illuminating these passionate scenes of pleasure.

"Pull your dick upward," she said. "I want you to put your hand on your balls."

He did precisely as she asked.

"Now squeeze them nice and tight for me," she said with a smile.

He did, and she watched as his balls grew tight and bulged outward. He moaned at the sensation of pressure.

"Harder," she commanded.

He squeezed tighter his very sensitive balls, and she could tell by the sounds that he was making that he was doing his best to comply.

"I really appreciate how obedient you are, Aiden. You are so naked right now, and I really get the impression that you are doing your best to obey me. It would please me if you showed me just how hard and tight you can take it. For me," she said.

He stood before her, completely naked, with one hand slowly stroking his cock for her, and the other gripping his balls as tightly as he could endure, providing both pleasure and pain for her amusement.

Emily listened to the sound of him breathing and the sound of his hand sliding back and forth along the shaft of his cock.

"Stop," she said, taking a deep breath.

She noticed the look of surprise on his face and asked him to come closer to her.

In a moment, he was inches from her face. She curled her hand around the back of his neck and brought his lips to hers.

She grabbed his cock with her other hand and began to mimic the movement she had been watching him make. She didn't need to prompt him; his hands roamed over her still-clothed body, and it wasn't long before he had his hand on her thigh, moving up her skirt. She leaned into him, holding on to him by his cock and the back of his head as his hand slid up between her legs.

He discovered that she had already removed her panties, and his middle finger slipped inside of her, causing her knees to buckle. She held on to him for support as he pleasured her clitoris.

Emily pulled her head back and looked at him with amazement, momentarily forgetting what she was doing with his cock, and now just holding on to it, squeezing it tightly in her hand as he set off fireworks of sexual pleasure between her legs. There were no words between them as he scooted her back, onto the desk, and lowered himself slowly onto his knees before her. Any uncertainty she may have felt evaporated when she saw the look of desire upon his face. He lifted her skirt and leaned into her, and she could feel his lips press against her inner thigh. His tongue, hot and wet, slid up her thigh and licked her between the legs. She leaned back, one hand on the desk and the other on the back of his head as she raised her legs and placed them over his shoulders and down his back.

There, that afternoon, she was certain of two things: One was that he had never done this before. Two was that he was going to have many, many opportunities to practice. She glanced down, and noticed that he was not only extremely hard, he was, perhaps, even harder than he had been minutes before. She could tell that he was incredibly turned on as he licked her, and though she had already decided that she would lose her virginity to him, she wasn't in any particular hurry, as she wanted to feel his tongue doing exactly what it was doing for as long as he was willing to do it. Which, as it turned out, was a very long time.

And so, for the first month or two of the semester, she would have Aiden visit her in her dorm room as often as every other day, and invariably, she would have him take off his clothes and masturbate in front of her. The two of them were the same age, but she had completely taken control of their relationship. She had made rules that he had to follow, mainly that he was no longer allowed to masturbate when she was not in his presence, but even then, she had become rather bossy, telling him what to do and when.

He had become infatuated with every part of it and was starting to realize that he would do anything for her.

Emily would ask him questions, mostly intimate in nature, and she came to feel thoroughly empowered to have Aiden do anything she wanted him to. Sometimes she just watched, making him pleasure himself in whatever way she chose. Other times, she would have him lie down on the bed and she would take him in her hand and jerk him off. On special occasions, she would allow him to kneel before her and lick her pussy, and she began to appreciate the fact that he seemed to be getting better and better at it.

The Book

Charlotte, Sarah, Juliette, Maya, Madison, and Emily sat in the living area of Sarah and Juliette's suite one afternoon with a computer monitor before them, displaying their newly built database.

"So, this is what I've got so far," Sarah began to explain. "Once you enter the website, you get this main page. It has a full set of photos, each represented in thumbnail size. If I click on any of the photos, then the full profile comes up, with each of the images in a little click-through here on the left, and all the information over here on the right. It has each guy's name, dorm room, stats—which include measurements and whatnot—then answers to personal questions, his preferences, et cetera."

"Show us their dicks!" Madison blurted out, breaking the silence.

Sarah laughed and Juliette smiled, and all of the girls continued their appraisal of each of the boys they had put through the interrogation process so far. Each of the photos featured the initiated boy standing completely naked and fully erect.

"I can't tell from these pictures who has the biggest dick," Madison pointed out, sounding irritated. "What the fuck, Emily," she teased.

Each of the photos were taken when the boy was fully erect, so their dicks were pointing toward the camera or slightly upward, which made a size comparison problematic.

"Is that important to you, Madison?" Emily asked with mock concern.

"Shut up!" Madison said with a laugh. "And yes, it *is* important to me. I want to know who has the biggest dick."

"Well, I want know who has the smallest dick," Maya replied with a sneer.

Juliette laughed at this, as she knew that Maya was somewhat preoccupied with the humiliation that was visited upon each of the boys during the interrogation. She seemed to specifically enjoy not only seeing the boys naked, but embarrassed as well—which, Juliette had to admit, was fun to watch, especially when it made the boys hard.

Sarah clicked on the one of the thumbnail photos to expand it. The focus of the photograph was the entirety of David McInnes's six-foot-one body, completely naked, in the boys' shower room of the school. He was standing beneath the showerhead with a bar of soap in his hand, and a spray of water was soaking every inch of his skin. The soap was causing foamy white bubbles to join the rivulets of water coursing over him, emphasizing every line, plane, and hardened masculine curve of his naked body.

"That was a super-cool idea to shoot him in the shower room. Boys tend to look good that way," Charlotte commented.

Sarah shrugged.

"I guess they're OK, but I see it all the time."

"Yeah, well, Emily here kicked this guy in the balls," Madison reported off-handedly.

"What?!" Maya exclaimed.

"No, I didn't!" Emily retorted. "It was my knee," she explained.

"Even better, I'd say," Maya observed.

"Well, at any rate, good photography, Em," Madison commented. "I mean, wow. You can see everything."

"Yeah, you can see his erect dick," Charlotte added. "I've been wondering who has the biggest dick in school."

"Is it him?" Juliette asked, pointing at the picture. "Because he looks pretty big."

"No, he's not the biggest," Sarah said. "There is a lot more to see—trust me."

Sarah clicked on the next photo, which was Steve Ahrmenson. Like David, he was in the middle of taking a shower, but he was turned almost to profile.

"Oh, I like this shot. You can see the curve of his butt," Maya observed. "And because of the water pouring down his body, it kind of looks like he is peeing," she mused.

"That's a really weird thing to think about," Charlotte replied.

Sarah clicked on the next photo, which revealed Darren Anders.

"Oh, this is funny." Charlotte laughed. "He posed for this picture right over here," she said, pointing to the other side of the room.

"He looks so naked!" Maya observed.

"I know, right? He is super cute. And that dick is even cuter," Sarah said.

"Well, we still haven't seen the biggest," Charlotte said.

"Yeah, but c'mon, that boy looks sexy," Maya protested.

"And you have a crush on him," Charlotte revealed.

"Yeah, well, we will have to come back to this page; I want to look at him longer," said Maya.

"You want to look at him with your hand in your panties!"

"Shut it!" Maya said, laughing.

But Charlotte wasn't wrong.

Sarah clicked on the next photo.

"What in the hell?!" Charlotte exclaimed. "I don't remember interrogating this guy."

"Yeah," Madison spoke up, "I did this one. Kind of like ... freelance."

"Well, good job, Madison. I think it's great that you had him pose as if he's masturbating. It almost looks like he isn't aware that you are taking the photo," Charlotte observed.

"Oh, he was totally aware I was taking the photo," Madison laughed.

"Well, it's totally hot thinking that he posed for you that way."

"Really? Because I think it's hotter if he didn't know she was taking a photo," Maya posited. "That would be so totally humiliating."

"You're a pervert!" Charlotte said with a chuckle.

"You're a slut!" Maya teased.

"Shut it, Maya! Anyway, I think the best part of this photo is seeing how he looks when he's jerking off. He's so into it, like he would be totally surprised if—"

"If you just walked into the room?" Maya interrupted, laughing. Yeah, I think he *would* be surprised. I'd tell him to keep going."

"Oh, and you call me a slut?" Charlotte quipped.

"You called me a pervert! Anyway, I just think it's hot. Also, in a way, we are watching him right now."

The next photo was taken in the courtyard, and it showed a boy from behind.

"Wait, who is this?" Charlotte asked. "Madison, is this another of your freelance photos?"

"Oh, it's Neil Densek," Emily admitted. "This one is a guy I photographed. He is on the punishment circle in the courtyard."

"What was he being punished for?" Charlotte asked. "Because that ass has clearly been beaten hard."

"Oh, you have to tell them the story!" Madison implored.

"He sent me this letter," Emily began. "It was this thing where he wrote to me after he got a punishment in Ms. Harwood's class. He was asking me if I would whip him, and it was just really inappropriate, so I showed the letter to Ms. Harwood. Anyway, he had to go before the dean."

"Oh my God," Charlotte said under her breath.

The other girls made similar sounds, as everyone knew how terrifying it was for the male students to have to go before the dean.

"I don't know what all happened there, but the next day in Rhetoric class, Neil was standing in position, facing the corner of the room, and he was completely naked."

Several of the girls chuckled appreciatively.

"And Ms. Harwood just carried on, ignoring him for most of the period. But at some point, she stopped lecturing and brought Neil to the front of the class, having him turn to face us. Then she made him read aloud the letter he had written. We could see that he was mortified, and it looked like he was going to cry."

Maya laughed.

"Then," Emily continued, "Ms. Harwood turned to me and asked me how many strokes of the rod I thought would be appropriate. I didn't know what to say, so I just said twenty. Ms. Harwood chastised me for being too lenient, so she doubled it to forty. She had him stand in position, facing the class, and delivered forty strokes of the birch rod, which we could tell was really brutal. Neil started crying, and when she was done, she had him face me and apologize. I just accepted the apology, so she had him thank me, but then he was made to stand at attention in the punishment circle in the courtyard for, like, twelve hours or something. So, I photographed him there."

Madison laughed and shook her head. Charlotte started clapping, which a few of the girls joined in on.

"That is amazing," Maya said. "Good job."

"And he has a cute butt—even more so because it's been whipped so thoroughly, but I still want to see his dick," Madison said.

Sarah clicked on the second photo of Neil, this one forward facing.

"Hmm," Madison murmured. "Nice pecs, nice abs, and—uh—nice ..."

"Yeah, it's not that big, but it's got personality," Emily said, laughing.

Madison chuckled.

"*Personality?* That's one way to describe it. So, you made his dick hard when he was on the punishment circle?"

"Yeah," Emily admitted. "I learned it from you."

"Oh my God, I'm so proud," Madison replied dreamily.

Sarah clicked on the next profile, and the photo that came up drew gasps and uproarious laughter.

"What the fuck is this?!" Madison cried out, laughing.

It was another photo taken in the shower room, and it was of the boy Sarah had nicknamed "Dick." He was on his knees with another boy's dick in his mouth.

"Yeah, this was an extracurricular activity I was interested in doing," Sarah admitted.

"That's Dick, right? The guy I saw when I visited you at work?" Charlotte inquired.

"Yeah, that's Dick, and he annoys me, so I made him take another guy's dick in his mouth. He was not happy about that."

Everyone had a laugh, partly due to the realization that this was now Dick's profile picture in the database, which all of the female students would be looking at.

Sarah turned the page to reveal Kyle Watson.

"This was the first guy we interrogated," Charlotte recalled. "The guy with the small dick."

"Right," Sarah confirmed, "so we are now ready to go live with the database. As soon as I publish this, every girl on campus can go on to it and look up any guy she wants to know more about."

"Fucking brilliant!" Charlotte exclaimed as she slow-clapped the group effort.

The Fallout

The Six gained a new level of respect among the student body upon the release of The Book. All of the girls at the school could now log in to the site to examine the boys they were curious about and read additional information about them. Perhaps the most popular part of the site was the crowdsourcing aspect. Each of the profiles could be edited, so that any additional information the girls had about any of the boys could be added.

Among the comments were the following:

"Mark went to my high school, and he was kind of a dick, but I think the Academy has been good for him. He is way more respectful, and he is definitely in better shape."

"Taylor is really shy, so it's nice to see him so completely exposed here. I am fascinated by how he looks in the photo where he is hard. He looks so naked it hurts!"

"This guy, Aaron, is an ASSHOLE. If you have the opportunity, report him for literally anything he does, because he deserves everything that's coming to him. Plus, he has a tiny dick, so fuck him."

"Daniel gave me a massage. He has the best hands, and he's really cool. He isn't really my type, so I'm just throwing that out there."

"Tyler gets his ass whipped all the time, so often that I think that he likes it. Can we please come up with a punishment that will actually be more effective?"

"Is anyone dating him? Cause I want him in my room. Doing my laundry. Naked."

The Academy administration either never found out about the website, or they didn't care. The female students had a lot of leeway, so they were unlikely to get in trouble for anything, and anything that could potentially act as a motivating force to condition the boys and make them more accepting of their place at the Academy was generally seen as a positive.

The impact the project had on the student body was both good and bad, depending on one's perspective. The comments and edits that were made by the female students dramatically enriched it as a resource, and soon, additional student profiles were added. The male students became aware of its existence, and soon, some of the guys who had not originally had a profile were endeavoring to have one added for them. Sarah remained the primary administrator, so she found that she had guys willing to do whatever she wanted in exchange for adding an entry for them. She had a virtual harem of young men doing favors for her, whether she asked them to or not, and she took full advantage of her newfound position.

The Barn

After Emily and Aiden had been meeting with each other in private for a few weeks, she asked him to help her with her photography. He agreed immediately and met with her at the appointed time.

"Thank you for helping me," she said as they began their hike.

It was a Saturday afternoon, and they were making the relatively short trek to what was simply referred to as "the barn," which had been built in the late 1800s before the land was sold to build the private academy that now occupied it.

"Yeah, no problem," he said with a broad smile. "I have seen your photography, and I think you are really talented. I am honored that you've chosen me to help out."

Ms. Strickland had mentioned that skin tone was one of the more difficult things to capture photographically, and Emily had decided she would master that, knowing exactly who she would recruit as her model.

"Thank you," she responded, "That means a lot to me. I have been working very hard at it."

When they arrived at the old barn, Aiden smiled in recognition.

"Ah, this place. I've been here before."

The barn was abandoned, and it had been a late-night hangout for occasional gatherings for decades. There had been a fire at one point, so the upper level had blackened, charred wood that revealed the open sky in some places. It had a very spooky appearance, and Emily had thought that it would make a fascinating backdrop for Aiden's naked body.

Emily suggested that they go up to the hayloft, which was a large airy space with lots of natural light. Emily looked around at the hayloft with fresh eyes. She had been there before, but that was generally at night. Now, daylight transformed the place, making it appear more magical.

"Why don't you stand there," she said, pointing to an area against a wooden railing. Sunlight poured over the area, and she felt that she could capture some good photographs with that much light.

He stood against the railing, facing her, and asked, "Like this?"

"No, silly," she said, taking the lens cap off and placing it in the camera bag. "I want to take pictures of you with your clothes *off,* not with your clothes *on.*"

He swallowed hard, and his face flushed red.

"Oh," he managed.

Emily stood before him, camera in hand.

"What's the matter?" she asked. "Are you scared?"

"A little," he replied, which was a bit of a lie. He was terrified. He had the sensation of standing on a cliff overlooking a deep lake, and he was being challenged to dive in. He placed his hands on his thighs, trying to stop them from trembling.

"That's OK," she said. "I don't mind if you are a little bit afraid to be photographed naked."

His head was swimming, and he had butterflies in his stomach. He marveled at the phrase "photographed naked." He had never even contemplated such a thing, but he knew that he was going to do as she asked, and so with some deliberation, he fumbled with the button on his cutoffs, then unzipped them. He kicked off his hiking shoes and pulled off his socks, then pulled his shorts off, throwing them to one side. Then he took off his shirt and paused for a moment. There was eye contact between them as he took hold of his underwear, slid it down his thighs, and pulled it off, tossing it into the pile of his other clothes.

Finally, Aiden stood before Emily and her camera, completely naked. She smiled at the sight. His body was thin and lean, yet nicely muscled, and his skin was beautifully tanned, with tan lines indicating the margins of his swim trunks. His cock had a curious attitude, which she examined through the lens of her camera. It was not hard, but it was definitely aroused. It looked thick and heavy, and the head of it was the size and shape of a plum, with the coloring of a pale cherry. She set the aperture of the camera based on the light reading, and then adjusted the focus. She set the frame size to take in the entirety of his body, and then took a deep breath.

"Are you ready?" she asked, looking at him above the camera viewfinder.

He smiled nervously and asked, "What if someone walks in here?"

"Then they see you naked, I guess," she said with a shrug of her shoulders.

Emily brought the camera to her eye and took the first photograph. The camera made a soft click, and that tiny mechanical sound changed everything. She had captured him, she realized. *There are few things as powerful as owning a photograph of someone when he is naked,* she thought to herself, *and now I have precisely that.* She had him lean against the wooden railing, as she made a few adjustments to the camera. Then she took another photograph. She peered at him over the camera and noticed with some delight that his dick was slowly becoming erect. She intuited that it was a bit embarrassing for him to be exposed this way, and it thrilled her to be documenting every moment of it.

"Um, who, by the way, will see these photographs?" he asked shyly.

"Whoever I show them to," she replied with a broad smile.

Aiden bit his lip nervously, and his cock grew harder.

Emily took another photograph, then moved closer to him and knelt down, which made it obvious that she was taking a photograph of his cock. The realization caused him to become fully erect, and she took another picture. The soft, hazy afternoon light made his skin glow, and she hoped that she had set her camera correctly to capture the way he looked. She noticed with some amusement that his erect cock threw a shadow across his hip.

"You have a really big dick," she commented, pointing her camera at her subject. "I think it will look nice in the photos I'm taking."

He blushed and thanked her for the compliment. She had him adjust his pose, asking him to look this way and that, put his arms up over his head, or place his hand alongside his cock. She took her time—a bit longer than she actually needed—enjoying each pose, perfecting it, and then savoring the moment when she pressed the button to capture the image. She also enjoyed prolonging the photo session, as every minute that he remained naked for her camera, the greater the chance was that someone might happen upon them. She knew this made him nervous, and she enjoyed the sexual tension that was so apparent in him.

Emily had Aiden move to an area that was bathed in sunlight and then kneel so that she could take a portrait of his face. It occurred to her as she was adjusting the focus on the camera that he was still completely naked for what was to be a headshot, which amused her. Moments later, she stepped back to take a full frontal shot of him kneeling on the floor.

"Put your hand on your cock," she said.

He did, carefully wrapping his hand around it, then looking up at her camera.

"Look that way," she directed, pointing. "Pretend that you don't know that I am here."

He did as she asked, and she snapped the picture.

"Play with your cock," she said, adding, "nice and slow." She took half a dozen photos from different angles, while he slowly stroked himself.

"Now stand up," she ordered, "and try to reach that beam over your head."

He arose, and standing on tiptoe, he could just reach it with the tips of his fingers. His body was stretched out before her, naked and hard. Emily told him to look upward, then took the photo.

"That's nice," she commented. "Is it difficult for you to hold that position?"

"A little," he said, and she could hear the strain in his voice.

"Well, maintain it for as long as you can," she said, "because it's a really nice pose, and I want to get a lot of pictures of your body in this position." She took another photo, then moved around behind him and took another, then a few in profile, before she told him to relax.

"Now go back over to the railing, and bend over it."

He bent forward over the railing, and she took some photos of his butt sticking out. She had him turn his head so that she could see his face in profile. She then had him spread his legs a bit farther apart, as there was something so vulnerable about his appearance in the photos when both his face and his ass were visible at the at the same time.

Then she stepped forward and took some time framing a shot of his butt, with his balls and cock visible below. This image proved to be difficult to capture just the way she wanted it, so she had to have him continue to make adjustments to his body position. It required some patience on his part as she tried different focal lengths and aperture settings, taking numerous photographs before she felt that she had captured the image just right.

At last, she put the camera aside, but left him in position. She smiled as she contemplated his predicament, bent over the railing for her to photograph and in such a vulnerable and exposed manner. She slowly approached him, pressing her hips against his backside and placing her hands on either side of his butt.

He laughed as she playfully thrust her hips against him.

"What are you doing?"

"I'm screwing you in the butt," she said, laughing. "What do you think I'm doing?"

"You don't have anything to screw with! You don't have a dick."

"Well, then we'll have to get me a dick. I think I'll take this one." She reached around his body and wrapped her hand around his cock, which had become soft, but thickened a bit in her hand.

"You already have this one," he said as he turned to face her.

He kissed her, and for a moment, they forgot where they were, but as they continued, they remembered that he was completely naked and they were in a place that they might be discovered, which was even hotter. She took his cock in her hand again, and felt that it was almost hard. She pulled away from him slightly and, while maintaining eye contact, she slid down to her knees. He leaned back against the railing, and she dropped her hands to her side, allowing his cock to stiffen before her open mouth. She looked up at him, as she slowly brought her lips to his cock, and watched him shudder as her tongue slid forward and touched him. His erect cock jumped at the sensation, and she waited a moment until it returned to her mouth. Then she moved her head forward, and her lips took the first inch of his cock between them. She brought her hands up to his muscular thighs, and she kept her eyes on his as her head slowly moved back and forth, feeling the shape of him on her tongue. It was several minutes before her lips reached the rim of his cock's head, and she took it in her mouth, sucking gently to increase the pressure. Every movement she made was slow and deliberate, letting him know that he wasn't going to come soon.

She was enjoying the fact that she had him naked in the barn and he was going to stay that way until she said otherwise. She wrapped her hand around his cock as she felt him getting close, sliding her hand back and forth on his shaft. She looked up at him and saw that he had his eyes closed, his head back, and he was completely overwhelmed by the pleasure she was delivering.

His body tightened and flexed, his hips pressing forward as he got closer and closer. She wondered if she was ready to make him come in her mouth. She felt some trepidation since she had never experienced that, but she had grown to love the taste of him in her mouth, and she didn't want to stop the pleasure she was giving him at the exact moment that it was at its peak. As she was contemplating this, the decision was suddenly made for her.

With his mouth open wide, he made an animalistic sound, his whole body tensed, and his come erupted in her mouth. She swallowed, and then he came again, and so she swallowed, and then he came again. Finally, she could feel his cock become less intensely hard, and the sounds he was making became sighs of content. She looked at him and found that he was looking at her. His hand gently brushed the side of her face. She sucked his dick, creating pressure as she pulled it out of her mouth, and it popped out and lay satisfied. He guided her up to his mouth and as they kissed, he could taste his come on her lips.

Later, lying on her bed in her dorm room, Emily thought about Aiden and all that had just transpired. She had taken off her skirt and pulled her panties down, and she now placed her fingers between her legs. She came to a decision about Aiden that made her come almost immediately.

The Photographs

Ms. Strickland called Emily into her office one afternoon. Pinned to the wall were some of the photos that Emily had been taking over the past month. None of them were of Aiden, but rather, they were an assortment of black-and-white pictures of various subjects, including a rusty rain barrel, a pair of old shoes, and a tree on the horizon.

Ms. Strickland stood up from her desk when Emily entered, and her long, slender fingers gestured toward the photos on the wall.

"These are all technically proficient, Emily," she said in her thin, dry voice, which still managed to sound threatening.

Emily understood that this was not the highest of praise.

"Still, I don't get any sense of you as the photographer," she continued. "Everything appears quite lifeless, and all that I see is an apathy toward your subject. So," she said as she turned to face Emily, "I want to see something with vitality, something that shows you as the artist photographing something that you care deeply about."

Emily looked at her shoes for a moment, wondering what she should do. Ms. Strickland was right. She had been taking photographs that meant nothing to her. They simply displayed a rudimentary skill in producing a picture. She looked up at the imposing woman.

"I have been taking some nude photographs. I think that they are much better."

Ms. Strickland's countenance changed.

"Oh, really?" she responded, mildly curious. "And whose skills as a model have you obtained for this enterprise?"

"Aiden's," Emily replied, and, indicating her schoolbag, added, "I have some in my portfolio now, if you would care to see them."

Ms. Strickland paused, examining her young student, then gestured to the wall.

"Yes, pin them to the wall here so that we can have a look at your work." She turned back to Emily and added, "Just a few of the ones you think are the best."

Emily spent the next minute or so hurriedly glancing through the photos, trying to select those which she thought not only showed her talent as a photographer, but also seemed appropriate to show her photography teacher.

Finally, impatiently, Ms. Strickland said, "Oh for heaven's sake, I am done waiting. If you can't decide, then put them all up."

And so Emily sheepishly began pinning each photo from her portfolio to the wall.

When she had a dozen or so mounted, Ms. Strickland declared, "Enough. We have enough examples here from which to make some observations."

She stood quite close to the wall, peering at each photo for some time before moving on to the next. At last, she began to speak, though she did so in a voice that betrayed her renewed estimation of her student.

"There are some who would say photographing an erect cock causes it to no longer be art and to necessarily be deemed pornography," she said dryly. "I think that is utter bullshit."

Emily was a bit embarrassed that she was pointing out that she had photographed Aiden's erection in the process. Ms. Strickland motioned to one of the photos with the plastic tip of her pen.

"In this photo, for instance, the subject is seen reaching up toward the beam that is overhead. The entirety of his movement, both physically and figuratively, is upward, and it would actually be distracting were his penis not doing the same. It appears aspirational, showing the desire of the model as he yearns to display himself to your satisfaction."

She turned to Emily and concluded, "This is why I wanted to meet with you. This," she gestured broadly, "is the kind of work you should be doing. I would like to assign you to complete a character study—with Aiden, if you wish, or another student, if you prefer."

Emily blushed, proud of herself and pleased by her teacher's words of encouragement. Although the thought of her being able to photograph some of the other boys intrigued her, she had become rather fond of Aiden.

As she began to collect her photographs, Ms. Strickland said, "Allow me to hold on to a few of these. I like to have examples of students' work for the purpose of inspiring other students."

Emily consented, and Ms. Strickland selected a few photos she thought were some of the better examples of her work. Emily then tucked the remainder into her portfolio.

She hurriedly made her way across campus, and met up with Aiden, who was waiting outside her dormitory. She took him by the hand and rushed up the stairs to her room.

"What's got you so excited?" he asked, her jubilant mood rubbing off on him.

She closed the door and threw the lock.

"I will tell you all about it later; now take off your clothes!"

He complied, and within moments he was standing before her, completely naked. She had taken her place, leaning against the edge of her desk, but instead of watching him play with himself, she extended her slender hand, pointing to the floor immediately between her feet.

"Come here," she said, "and get on your knees."

He did as she commanded.

She looked down on his smiling face and noticed that he was fully erect. She placed her hand on the back of his head and pulled him toward her body. Aiden slid his hands up her thighs, lifting her skirt as she guided his face between her legs. He slid her panties down to the floor, and she stepped out of them. He kissed her gently between her legs, the soft, small bush of hair tickling his nose as he pressed his lips to hers. She was dripping wet in her excitement, and Aiden slowly, gently lapped up her wetness. He kissed and licked her, listening to the sounds she made in response. She leaned back on the desk, propping herself up with one hand, while the other combed through Aiden's hair, gently guiding him as he explored her pussy with his tongue.

Juliette, Antony, and Maya

After the "interrogation" in the old, dilapidated cottage in the woods, Juliette had established a relationship with Antony that fit her interests perfectly. First, she'd laid down some ground rules with Antony. He was to show up when she requested and generally be available for whatever she might wish to do with him. Sometimes she just had him go down on her as a break from studying, and occasionally she would tie him up and whip him, both as stress relief and to continue his training. Sometimes she would have him fuck her.

Now, in the living room of her suite, she had just decided to tie a blindfold across Antony's face, when the door suddenly opened and her roommate, Maya, entered.

Maya stopped, speechless, as she took in what was happening. She observed Juliette in the process of blindfolding Antony, and she stood frozen for a moment, unsure of what to do.

"I guess I should have knocked," Maya said, trying not to giggle.

A few days earlier, Juliette had shown Maya a photo of Antony with a length of rope tied around his balls. The rope was taut, as though it were being held by someone just out of frame of the photo.

"Are you holding the rope that's tied around him?" Maya had asked.

"Yeah, nice and tight!" Juliette had responded, laughing.

"So, you really *do* have him by the balls," Maya had observed. "I'm impressed!"

"Oh, you don't know the half of it!"

Now, Maya was seeing firsthand the depth of Antony's submission to Juliette.

"Well, hello!" Juliette said between bursts of laughter.

"Um, hi," Maya returned. She would have been embarrassed, but she could see that Juliette wasn't, and she could also see that Antony *was*. He was blindfolded, so he couldn't see her, but she could see everything, including the fact that he was blushing from embarrassment. She had never seen a guy look so naked, and she was impressed with sight of her roommate standing over him, so clearly in control.

"Sorry, I just needed to get some things. I can come back later?" Maya asked.

"It's fine," Juliette said with a laugh. "Go ahead and do whatever you need to do."

This put Maya more at ease.

"I just need to get some books and my gray sweatshirt. Then I will leave you two alone to do ... whatever you are going to do," she said with a wink.

"Totally fine," Juliette responded. "I was just about to whip Antony."

"I would love to see that," Maya inadvertently murmured.

"You should watch," Juliette suggested in a playful tone. "I think it will be humiliating for him to have another girl witness his punishment."

"But how are you going to ..." Maya began, trailing off as she considered the prospect.

Juliette laughed, seeing her roommate's confusion.

"I'm going to whip him across the dick," Juliette explained.

Maya laughed.

"Well, you won't miss," she said as a joke, indicating the size of Antony's dick. She couldn't help but notice that he had an erection, which, she thought, must certainly be embarrassing for him. And since he was blindfolded, she felt no embarrassment in staring directly at it. "Doesn't that hurt?" she inquired.

"Yeah, I'm going to make it hurt a lot," Juliette replied with a smile, "but he loves it because it allows him to show me obedience. Isn't that right?" she asked Antony, her hand tousling his hair.

"Yes, Miss," he replied softly.

Maya leaned back on the edge of her desk, and said, "OK, I'm curious."

Juliette took hold of her horse whip and brought it up between Antony's legs, placing the tip alongside his erect cock.

"Now, you are not going to embarrass me, are you? You are going to take a whipping with an attitude of enthusiastic obedience, right, Antony?"

"Yes, Miss," he replied softly, with an obvious respect for her. Although it was going to be humiliating for him to be whipped across the dick in front of Maya, he was proud of the fact that Juliette wanted to whip him.

Juliette brought the whip up between his legs and pressed the tip against the base of his cock. Maya held her breath, fascinated by what she was seeing. Juliette brought the whip back a few feet, and Maya bit her lip in anticipation. She was leaning back against the desk, her hands gripping the smooth, rounded edge of the desktop as she took in the sight of Antony tied naked to the chair, and her roommate Juliette wielding a sinister-looking whip. Juliette flicked her wrist, and the whip followed, smacking Antony on the base of his cock. He gasped and his body lurched, pulling at his restraints. His naked dick vibrated from the impact. Maya burst out laughing, both from surprise and delight at Antony's reaction to Juliette's action.

Juliette gave a soft chuckle, amused by her roommate's response to the situation. Their eyes met for a moment, and Juliette read the admiration in Maya's expression. Juliette wondered if she had become jaded, as Antony was not the first boy she had whipped, and she no longer had the feeling of surprise that Maya had. This is not to say that she didn't love whipping a boy, as she absolutely adored it—both the sadistic thrill of it and the rush of feeling powerful in dominating a naked boy with a hard-on.

She brought the whip back again and used it to slap Antony's cock a bit higher up on its shaft. Again, he gasped, a sound that became a soft moan, and his body involuntarily pulled at its restraints.

Maya licked her lips and exhaled audibly as the pleasure of witnessing Antony's humiliating punishment washed over her. It occurred to her that she would never look at him the same way after this, with the thought of *Yeah, I saw that guy naked, getting whipped across the dick* in her head.

For his part, Antony had never felt so embarrassed. He wasn't ashamed of the fact that Juliette could do anything she wanted to him, but to have it witnessed by another person made him feel extraordinarily exposed. And far beyond that, to have his dick whipped in front of an audience was thoroughly terrifying. But Juliette had secured him to the chair so there was nothing he could do about it. He wouldn't want to anyway, as he was so incredibly turned on by everything Juliette was doing to him. He wanted nothing but to please her, and he wanted to be allowed to lick her at every opportunity he was presented with, so he did as he was told.

Juliette brought the whip back and paused, waiting. Maya noticed that she was purposely making Antony wait, expectantly, for each stroke of the whip. She held her breath, her eyes wide in fascination, taking in the whip, Antony's erect cock, and the expression on his face. Her gaze was drawn to the movement of the whip and the nakedness that was its target, but she tried to maintain her attention on his face as the whip struck him.

This was the case for Juliette as well, as the moment the whip made contact with him, she wanted to observe his reaction. And so it was that every time Antony's cock was whipped, both girls were watching his face as he yelped, moaning in pain, yet still undeniably turned on.

The whip had been inching upward and now it was being held against the tip of his cock. Maya took note of this and inhaled in anticipation. Juliette noticed that Maya was appreciative of how much more sensitive the tip of the dick was, and she was intensely interested in what would happen.

Juliette turned toward Maya and shot her a *Watch this* look. She drew the whip back, and all three of them waited in anticipation—two in curious excitement and one in abject terror. Finally, Juliette flicked her wrist hard, and the whip spanked the tip of Antony's cock with a satisfying smack. He cried out, his body pulling at his restraints, and Maya couldn't help but laugh at his predicament. This made Juliette laugh as well, and though the two girls might have thought that perhaps it was a bit cruel to laugh at Antony's expense, they couldn't help themselves. Besides, they were enjoying playing with their victim, and he was endlessly turned on by all of this, so they felt that he probably deserved the punishment he was getting. And so they continued to laugh as Juliette proceeded, now focused on the tip of his cock.

Eventually, Juliette turned to Maya and offered the whip to her.

"Would you like a turn?"

Maya hesitated, nervously eyeing the long, sinister whip.

"Really? Is ... that OK?"

Juliette laughed.

"If I say it is, then yes, it is. Go ahead," and with that, she gestured with the whip, holding it out for Maya to take.

Maya reached out and took the whip in her hand. Juliette smiled warmly, pleased that she didn't feel jealous in any way. She knew that Antony would be devotedly licking her after Maya had gone, and it would significantly deepen Antony's respect for her, in that she had, apparently, the power to extend her domination of him to allow another girl to whip him.

The two girls traded places, and as Juliette leaned back against the desk, watching the scene before her, Maya took her position alongside Antony's naked, captive body. She observed the rope that secured his ankles to the front legs of the chair and his hands to the back of the chair, which forced him to remain exposed and vulnerable. She glanced at his face, blindfolded and expectant, and suppressed a giggle as she slid the whip up, along his inner thigh, bringing it to rest against the tip of his erect cock. She paused and took a deep breath. All three waited in silence for some moments in anticipation of what was to come.

Though it wasn't lost on Maya that this guy belonged to Juliette, and, in fact, it had never been clearer than it was at this moment, still, she did think he was kind of cute. It gave her a tingling sensation to hold the whip when he was tied up and so very, very naked. She brought the whip back and let him have it. There was an audible slap as the whip made contact with the tip of his cock, and Antony made a desperate moaning sound. Juliette watched in fascination, feeling a voyeuristic thrill as Antony took his whipping. At one point, Maya let the whip slide down the length of his shaft, bringing it to rest against his naked balls. Juliette read her intention.

"Hold on," Juliette said, and retrieved a length of rope. She took his balls in her hand and tied the rope around them. Then she took the other end of the rope and pulled it straight upward. This served to present his balls in a more accessible, more vulnerable way. She pulled the rope tight and ordered Antony to open his mouth. She held the taut rope between his teeth and told him to bite down. He complied. She stepped back and instructed him to keep the rope tight.

Maya had been watching with deep curiosity everything that Juliette was doing, and now that she had accomplished her task, Maya marveled at the effect it had produced. Antony's balls, previously between his legs, were now pulled upward and directly in line with the whip. She could appreciate the irony that he was being made to hold them there himself by keeping the rope nice and tight between his teeth. Maya took her time in bringing the whip back in place between his thighs. She held it there, pressed gently against his balls, and allowed the anticipation to build. Both girls examined the predicament that Antony was in, and they couldn't help but laugh at what was coming next.

Maya made little circles with the whip, caressing its sensitive target in a rather malicious way, teasing Antony with the fear that was building in the pit of his stomach. She began with a gentle little tap, practically making a mockery of the punishment that was to come. Both girls had to laugh when he jumped, preemptively, at the subtle slap. Juliette reminded Antony to keep the rope tight, so that his balls were conveniently positioned for Maya to whip. She complimented him on his obedience and indicated to Maya that she should feel free to whip him hard. Maya laughed at the suggestion, agreeing to do just that. She slowly pulled the whip away from his body, then, with a snap of her wrist, flicked his balls with the whip. The sound he made with the rope held clenched between his teeth was delightful, and his body jolted from the pain, which caused Juliette and Maya to burst into laughter.

"Oh, poor baby!" Juliette cried out in a mocking tone. "Did the whip hurt your balls?!"

"Maybe I shouldn't whip him so hard!" Maya commented in a tone that made it clear she was joking.

"Oh, for sure, much softer this time!"

Maya whipped him again, harder, and his reaction was even better.

"Yeah, that was good," Juliette offered. "Nice and soft, just like that!"

Maya whipped him harder still, and he cried out in pain. The girls laughed again, enjoying the cruel game.

Later that afternoon, after Maya had handed the whip back to Juliette and had taken her leave, Juliette had Antony go down on her. For over an hour, he worshipped her with his tongue. She was lying on the bed, with her hips on the edge and her feet on the floor, a collection of pillows behind her head. Antony was on his knees on the floor, and his hands were on her hips. For the first fifteen minutes, he kissed her passionately, occasionally lapping up her wetness and reveling in the taste of her, then slowly licking her up and down.

Propped up on the pillows, Juliette had an ideal spot from which to observe him serving her pleasure. She threw her head back with the waves of ecstasy emanating upward through her body. While Antony slowly brought her to orgasm, Juliette thought about his whipping. She recalled how his back had arched and his mouth had flown open in a guttural moan, his body held tightly by its restraints. She thought about how he'd waited patiently, anticipating what was coming next. She thought about how thrilling it had been to watch him, tied up naked, taking a whipping from her roommate. And she thought about how hard his cock had been throughout. As she was about to come, she replayed in her mind how the whip had landed, over and over, across his most intimate, sensitive parts, and how he'd recognized her authority to do as she'd pleased with him. Finally, as she began to orgasm, she thought about how turned on he always was to serve her, no matter what she did to him.

After having made her come, Antony began softly kissing her upper thighs, eventually licking her to another orgasm.

After she'd come for a second and then a third time, Juliette pulled Antony up off the floor and onto her bed, where she guided his cock between her legs. He began to fuck her slowly, in part because his cock was sore from the whipping. Also, because he was moments from coming after the long, erotic torment she had given him that day. It took over a minute for him to enter her fully, but then he began to slowly increase the pace, fucking her in long, sensual thrusts.

She slid her hands up his chest and pulled him closer to her. He kissed her, deeply and passionately, as he buried his cock inside of her.

"What did you enjoy most, having your cock whipped or your balls whipped? she whispered.

"Um, licking you," he replied with a smile.

"Oh, you'll get a whipping for that, smart-ass!"

"I would, actually, like a spanking from you. Across my butt."

"Really, now. With what?"

"Your bare hand."

"Hmmm. So you want a spanking with my bare hand? Because that can be arranged."

"Thank you, Miss," he said as he began licking and sucking on her nipples. She thought about spanking him as her hands made their way down his body to cup his butt cheeks. She grabbed and squeezed them as he thrust into her. At last, he came inside of her with an intensity she hadn't experienced before. His body was trembling as the last of his come emptied into her.

After he gave her a nice, long massage, she allowed him to kiss and lick her ass as a reward for having been so obedient. She knew that he loved serving her with his tongue, and that he adored licking her everywhere, especially her ass, so she let him continue as she informed him, "Your spanking will be tomorrow. I look forward to it."

Ryan

It was late afternoon on Friday, and Emily was examining the photos of her fellow students. Each student was showing the results of his or her latest assignment. The challenge had been to create a set of photographs that would represent a self-portrait. For her part, Emily created a series of product shots of the contents of her purse. It was a bit tongue-in-cheek, and rather clever, so it was well-received among the students.

Emily had her eye on some of the other offerings. She was intrigued by David's set of photos, which featured him blindfolded and tied up in different situations, some of them outdoors. She was unsure of his intent, but she found his photo set quite compelling. She also found David himself to be quite interesting. She had to suppress a laugh whenever she had any interaction with him, as she couldn't help but think about slamming her knee into his balls on the very first day of the class.

She was also fascinated by Ryan's photos in which he appeared nude. The pictures weren't pornographic; in fact, his dick wasn't visible in any of the pictures, but he was fully naked, nonetheless. His body was much nicer than she would have thought. He was tan with a nice muscular build and brown hair that had natural highlights from the sun. There was an innocence to his boyish cuteness. As class was ending, she gathered up her own photos and slipped them into her portfolio. She noticed Ryan gathering together his belongings.

"Hi, Ryan. Your photos were really interesting this week."

"Thank you, Miss. I really liked yours too. I thought that was a really interesting approach to addressing the concept of identity."

"Thank you. Of course, it didn't take as much bravery as showing nude photos."

Ryan blushed.

"Would you have any interest in helping me with the photo assignment for next week?" Emily asked.

"Oh, um, sure, Miss. Do you have an idea for what you might want to do?"

"Well, the assignment is to take photos that respond to this week's assignment, so I would be taking photos of you that respond to the way that you presented your public image this week."

"OK, that makes sense. Are you thinking they would be nude photos, Miss?"

Sensing Ryan's nervousness, Emily laughed.

"I guess we'll have to see, won't we?"

Measurement

"So, tell me about the measurement book," James asked Madison while sitting on the end of her bed after class. Though he had been blindfolded when she had first measured him, he had heard Emily slip one day, mentioning something about Madison's "Dick Diary." By that point in time, he knew her well enough to know that this was exactly the kind of thing she would do.

"What measurement book?" she replied in her manner of being exasperating.

"You know. When I first came over to your room, you said that you were measuring me, but I was blindfolded so I wasn't really sure what that was all about. Now, apparently, I have learned that you keep a kind of diary about the subject."

"Emily!" Madison exclaimed, shaking her fist. Then she turned to James with a sweet and innocent look on her face. "I love big cocks, and I want to know just how big they are. You know, like, for science."

Madison laughed as James raised an eyebrow.

"OK, science lady, how big am I?"

"Oh, shut up. Every guy knows how big he is."

"Yes, but I don't know how big you think I am."

Madison stared straight ahead, her eyes widening as she slowly separated her hands farther and farther apart.

"Big," she said.

"OK, never mind," James relented.

"Oh, well, *OK,*" Madison said as she reached over and opened her bedside drawer. She pulled out her moleskin notebook and opened it to a marked page. "You are ten and one-quarter inches. That would be almost exactly twenty-six centimeters in metric," she informed him. "And you are just shy of six and a half inches in circumference, which is about sixteen and a half centimeters."

She slapped the book shut in a show of finality, but James protested.

"Wait, you can't be telling me that I am the only guy you have measured. You must have other measurements in that book."

Madison paused, then exhaled, watching the expression on his face closely.

"I do."

"So? Can I know what they are?"

"Why so interested?" she asked conspiratorially.

"Hey, if I am in it, I want to know where I am, you know, ranking-wise."

Madison stared at him, a look of amusement on her face.

"You have the biggest fucking cock I have ever seen, James."

She leaned forward and kissed him, and he could feel her body begin to melt into his, but then she sat up again.

"And take it from me," she said as she gestured with the notebook, "that means something."

She put the notebook aside, pushed him down onto the bed, then threw her leg over him to straddle his chest. She lifted the hem of her dress, revealing herself to him.

"I have this tiny pussy, James, and yet, I have this fascination—no, this *need* for big fucking cock. You know what that means?"

"That we can't have sex?" James asked, his voice quiet.

"No, James, it means that it would hurt like hell, so I need you to learn to come from licking my pussy."

"Wait, what? Really?"

"Yes, really," and she became softer, and quieter. "I want to watch you come while you are licking me."

She took a deep breath, then became still, watching as James contemplated all that she had told him. She waited for him to respond, searching his face as he thought about what he was going to say.

"Do you mind if I take off my pants, Miss?" James asked.

They had more or less dropped the Academy-mandated use of the honorific, "Miss," so it disarmed her to hear it.

"I thought you would never ask," she replied, and immediately began unzipping his pants before pulling them down.

There was a brief melee of clothing being yanked off and thrown about the room, and when they were completely naked, he cautiously took her hand and placed it between his legs. Madison eyed him curiously, gently closing her fingers around his balls and gripping him firmly. She noticed that his eyes glazed over with desire as she applied pressure, and so she began to massage his balls, slowly increasing the pressure. He placed his hands on her legs in a way that suggested she mount him in reverse, with her pussy in his face. She followed his movements and inhaled sharply as she felt his tongue stroke her clit. She began to slowly ride his tongue, holding on to his balls like a horn on a saddle.

"Oh, fuck, James," she whispered. "Can you come like this?"

He didn't answer, but instead, continued to follow the movement of her body. He responded to every breath, every gasp, and every thrust until she came, her body shuddering as her orgasm overwhelmed her. Simultaneously, she bore down, squeezing his balls in her grip. And then she got her answer.

The Waterfall

"Where are we going, Miss?" Ryan asked.

He had brought a pair of swim trunks as she had advised him to do, so he assumed that they were going to the lake, which was a bit of a hike.

"It's a surprise!" Emily replied. She was wearing a pair of hiking boots, a navy-blue skirt, and an oversized T-shirt tied in a knot at the waist, with its sleeves rolled up. Her hair was tied back in a ponytail, and she had her large camera bag over her shoulder.

"Actually," she said, stopping, "this bag is rather heavy. Would you mind carrying it?"

"Of course not," he replied with a broad smile. He took the bag and placed the strap over his shoulder and across his bare chest. He was wearing a pair of hiking boots and a pair of long shorts over his swim trunks. She observed the leather strap of the camera bag lying tight across his smooth, tanned chest, and it excited her for reasons she couldn't explain. They resumed their hike, which took up much of the next hour. As they made their way to their destination, they amused themselves by comparing the teachers at the academy to different animals, noting that some were like walruses, some were like storks, and their favorite teacher was most like an old lion.

They could hear the water burbling and splashing on the rocks as they drew close. As they came around a bend in the trail, they saw it: a twenty-foot waterfall splashing onto the smooth, giant boulders below.

"Whew ..." Ryan said, more of an exhalation than a word. "This is beautiful! How in the world did you find this, Miss?"

"I was looking at a topographical map," Emily replied, "and I noticed that this river had a higher elevation than the lake."

"So, I guess you are pretty smart, Miss," he said in admiration.

"Yes, I am!" she responded.

He felt his head swimming until she broke the spell by saying, "Now take off your clothes, and go stand under the waterfall."

"But I brought swim trunks ..." he said in bewilderment.

"Yeah," she said with a laugh, taking her camera bag back from him, unzipping it, and extracting her camera. "I changed my mind. I think it will make for a better photo if you're nude while being splashed with water."

"Very, very cold water," he mused.

"Oh, come on," she chastised him. "Are you scared? Afraid that you might get wet?"

He laughed and wasn't entirely truthful when he said, "No, I'm sure I will be fine."

Ryan took off his hiking boots and socks, then unbuttoned his shorts and dropped them to the ground. He took a quick look around, a bit nervous, then slipped off his swim trunks.

Emily watched him as he did this, feeling the same exhilaration she always did when he stripped naked at her command. This was particularly satisfying, as he was standing in full sunlight. She brought her camera to her eye and snapped a photo. His body looked brilliant against the wooded backdrop. He appeared like a natural part of the environment, as though he had never worn clothes at all. His cock looked thick and heavy, swinging lazily as he made his way over the large rocks toward the waterfall. She followed him and noted with a bit of a thrill that he was moving farther and farther away from his clothing. She knew the waterfall was fairly remote and not a lot of people knew about it, but it was fully out in the open, where anyone might happen upon them at any moment.

There was a narrow trail that led up to the side of the waterfall, and she watched as he climbed it, stopping just a few feet from the water. When he turned to face her, she saw that his body was glistening with drops of water from the spray that emanated from the splash as the water hit the rocks.

"Oh fuck, it's *cold!*" he exclaimed.

She snapped a photo of him.

"Come on! I want to see the water running over your body."

His dick did not look very big, which she assumed was due to the temperature of the water, but she thought it looked cute like that, so she took another photo. He turned, and with determination, stepped into the edge of the waterfall. His mouth flew open in shock and surprise, and his exclamation could only be described as a loud whoop.

Emily was happy she had her camera ready. She snapped a photo of his reaction as the water poured over his body in a deluge. He leaned against the smooth rock, and threw his hands up over his head, posing for her camera. She was amused by the look of him, his lean muscular body, tanned and naked, with his dick looking smaller than she had ever seen it. She kept taking photos and wondered if she could make his cock hard in this situation. He seemed to be slowly acclimating to the temperature of the water and appeared more relaxed as she continued to photograph him. She lowered her camera and peered at him.

"I want to see you touching yourself," she called out.

He looked at her with a lustful desire, amazed by the wonderfully sexy games she continued to invent. He wordlessly complied and began playing with his cock.

She took photos of him masturbating under the waterfall and noticed with delight that his cock was becoming harder as he played with it. Within minutes, she had what she wanted: he was leaning back against the rock, water pouring over his naked body, and he was fully erect. She told him to place his arms up, over his head, and push his hips forward. He did so, and she took what she felt was an amazing photo. The water splashed against his thick, hard cock, and the expression on his face was a haze of sexual desire.

"Put your hand around your balls," she requested, "and hold them so that they get sprayed by the water."

He brought his hand down between his legs and wrapped his hand around his balls as she had told him to do. She watched the expression on his face as the hard spray of cold water made contact. She took a photo and told him to remain as he was while she took a few more photos of him in this pose.

She then pulled out a plastic bag and tucked her camera inside of it.

"Let's go behind the waterfall," she suggested. There was a large alcove behind the curtain of water, which would comfortably fit the two of them.

"OK," he said, agreeably. It was a few steps farther to duck below the curtain of water, which were over quickly for both of them, and they found themselves in the small alcove behind the waterfall.

"Wow!" she exclaimed. "You weren't kidding; that water is *cold!*"

"Oh, but you were OK with me standing in that water?" he said, laughing.

"Yeah, well, look. There are different rules for the two of us. I make the rules, and you follow them, mister," she said, teasing him.

"OK, Miss," he replied. "And what are the rules now?"

With a devious smile, she placed her camera on a dry ledge and said, "Get on your knees."

She approached him and stood inches from his face. His hands slid up her thighs, and he lifted her skirt. He slid her underwear down and took them off. He then placed his tongue between her legs and began to lick her.

Emily was fascinated by the difference between Aiden's tongue and Ryan's. They were both fairly good at being attentive to her, following her cues to go faster, slower, harder, softer, and they had both figured out how to lick her clit, but they were also very different. How they were different, she couldn't say, but it occurred to her that she would need to have both of them lick her pussy, preferably one after the other, to really appreciate the difference. And with that thought, imagining them taking turns between her thighs, she had her first orgasm, which felt as thunderous and as wet as the waterfall beside them.

Emily's Decision

"I have something to admit to you, Aiden," Emily revealed, with a curious tone in her voice. "I showed Ryan your photos from the barn. I mean, I showed a few of them in my photography class, you know, as part of the work I am expected to do for class. I displayed some of the photos I took that day and got really high marks for them. I also got a lot of compliments from the other students. But I showed Ryan the full set."

"Oh! Ryan?" he asked with astonishment. He'd realized that she could show the pictures to whomever she wanted to, but he hadn't realized that Ryan would care to see them.

"Yeah, I was interested in knowing what he would think of them."

"I see," he replied, blushing a little. "And what did he say about them?"

"He was fascinated, actually. He studied each photo intently. Part of his interest was due to the fact that I'd just taken some photos of him as well."

She studied Aiden's face as she gave him this information.

His face flushed red, and he experienced an awkward feeling of jealousy. However, Emily could see that he was intrigued, possibly even aroused.

"So, I mean, what does that mean as far as you and I are concerned?" Aiden asked warily.

"Oh, are you jealous, silly?"

She took his face in both of her hands and gave him a kiss.

"I still want to take photos of you. And I want to do all the other things as well," Emily said, stroking his hair. "I want to play with you, and I want to have sex with you."

Aiden looked at her hopefully.

"You do?"

"Yes, Aiden. I love your body, and I love the way that you touch me and the way that you kiss me and the way that you lick me." She kissed him again. "But I want Ryan too. I want both of you."

Emily observed how her words affected Aiden. She noticed that his eyes grew wide and his breathing quickened. He showed signs of arousal.

"I want both of you at the same time," Emily revealed, a tone of finality in her voice.

"So," Aiden replied, then went silent as he considered the impact of Emily's words.

"Yes?" Emily prompted.

"I'm not sure what to say," Aiden said, his voice strained.

"Right, which is why I am prompting you," Emily explained softly. "Say yes."

Aiden sat quietly for a moment, thinking; then he turned to look into her eyes.

"Yes," he said.

Emily pulled him to her and kissed him, and he could feel the passion that was building within her, just waiting to be unleashed.

Juliette and Maya's Decision

"So, I've been thinking," Juliette mentioned, pausing with a cup of yogurt in one hand, her spoon held aloft in the other.

"Oh, good," Maya replied. "Trouble."

Juliette laughed.

"Yeah, trouble. I just keep thinking how much I loved the way that Antony responded to the two of us, and I have been wondering ..."

"Go on," Maya implored.

"Well, what if we do that again? And maybe, what if we make that a thing? Like, we kind of share?"

"How do you mean?"

"It was just so fun when we kind of tag-teamed him."

"I loved the humiliation of it. For him, I mean."

"Yeah, I know, you really like humiliating guys, and I like watching Antony get humiliated. It's perfect."

"Perfect," Maya repeated, a conspiratorial look on her face. "I'm in."

"OK, check this out," Juliette said as she pulled out her phone and clicked on a video she had recorded. The video showed that she had mounted a large, lubricated dildo with a suction cup base to a straight-backed chair. She had Antony sit down on the chair naked, and she kept the camera on him as he took in every inch of the massive dildo.

"This is so awesome," Maya observed. "I love it that you have him take it up the ass."

Then Antony began masturbating in the video.

"Can you make it play in slow motion?" Maya asked.

Juliette pressed a button, which made him appear to masturbate even slower and emphasized the erotic nature of the subject matter.

"See, I think it would be way more intimidating for him to have to do this in front of both of us—and therefore, more fun," Juliette observed.

"I think it would be totally embarrassing for him," Maya replied, laughing. "Which is why we should definitely do it. I think it would be fun to watch him strip naked and masturbate for us when he is really intimidated and he feels really self-conscious and naked."

The video continued, but Juliette and Maya turned their attention to discussing the logistics of enacting their idea. Juliette wondered aloud if he should be blindfolded, but Maya thought that it would be better if he wasn't. By the time the video ended, Juliette and Maya had a made a plan.

When Antony arrived at Juliette and Maya's suite a few days later, he wasn't surprised to see that Maya was there, sitting next to Juliette on the sofa. But he *was* surprised when Juliette told him to take off his clothes. The girls could see that he was nervous, intimidated by the fact that they were both sitting there so expectantly.

"Go ahead," Juliette said. "We want to see you naked."

Antony removed his clothing as directed and waited.

Juliette and Maya were openly staring at him and, aside from a few giggles to each other, saying nothing.

He remained standing there in the center of the room, awkwardly, wondering what was going to happen.

"What do you want me to do, Miss?"

That caused both of them to laugh, and Juliette turned to Maya.

"Hmmm, what do you think we should have him do?" Juliette asked.

"I don't know," Maya replied. "What do you think we should have him do?"

"I don't know," Juliette replied, laughing.

"He's a pretty good size," Maya mused. "I wonder how big he is."

"Should we measure him and find out?" Juliette asked.

"I don't know. That would be interesting to know, you know, numerically. It would provide a benchmark for comparison."

"Oh, yeah, that could be useful," Juliette replied.

Juliette removed from a desk drawer her hardwood ruler and stood before Antony. Maya took her place beside Juliette to watch. Juliette placed one end of the ruler against Antony's body at the base of his erection and used her other hand to press the shaft against the smooth surface of the ruler.

"It looks like it's a bit longer than eight inches," Maya said. "I wonder if it would be longer if he was even harder?"

"Possibly," Juliette replied. To Antony, she directed, "Make it harder so we can measure it."

Juliette and Maya both took a step back to watch as he placed his hand on his cock and began to slowly move it back and forth along the shaft.

"That is kind of fascinating," Maya observed, "how his foreskin slides back and forth."

"Yeah, it has taught me a lot about the level of control you can have over a boy. I have come to understand that I can do pretty much anything I want with him, all because he gets hard when he is with me."

"Do you want to measure him again to see if he's harder?" Maya asked.

"Yeah, OK."

Juliette told Antony to place his hands at his sides. Juliette placed the ruler in the same way she had before.

"Oh my gosh—it's almost eight and a half now!" Juliette exclaimed, laughing. "He *does* get even harder!"

Juliette tapped the wooden ruler against her palm a few times, enjoying the menacing sound it made.

"Will he stand still if you spank his balls with the ruler?" Maya inquired.

"Of course," Juliette replied.

Juliette turned toward Antony.

"You'll be a good boy and stand still for us, won't you?"

His face blushed and he began to tremble.

His mouth was dry as he replied, "Yes, Miss."

"Good, but I am not going to use the ruler," Juliette declared, piquing Maya's curiosity.

Juliette reached into her closet and produced an extraordinarily impressive long wooden paddle.

Juliette had been waiting for the right opportunity to use the heavy fraternity paddle. Her brother had received it in college and had given it to Sarah for whatever purpose she might have for it. She had joked about the fact that this paddle had seen a lot of naked boy butts, and she'd brought it with her to school, guessing it might come in handy. She thought it would be fun to paddle the boys, making them bend over and take a hard spanking, but now she had a better use for it.

"That is fucking awesome," Maya exclaimed, clearly impressed.

"I know, right?" Juliette agreed, then turned her attention to Antony.

"Place your hands on your head and stand with your legs spread apart," she demanded.

He complied, and the fear and anticipation that he felt was evident, to the amusement of the two girls.

Juliette placed the flat, smooth, wooden surface of the paddle against his balls.

"Are you ready?" she asked.

"Yes, Miss," he replied, his voice barely a whisper.

"Are you sure? Because this is probably going to hurt."

Maya laughed at the fact that she was clearly taunting him, allowing his anticipation to grow.

"Well, his dick is still really hard, so I guess he's as interested in finding out how much it will hurt as we are," Maya observed.

"Yeah, his dick *is* really hard. Maybe I should spank him a bit harder than I had intended," Juliette mused.

After teasing him a bit longer, she drew the paddle back and delivered a nice, hard smack between his legs, making contact with both of his balls simultaneously. Juliette and Maya studied his face as the sensation of erotically charged pain coursed through him. His knees buckled, but he remained standing. Maya burst out laughing at his reaction, and Juliette couldn't help but be amused.

"Fascinating," she said with a soft chuckle. "Now let's see what happens if I do it harder." She drew the paddle back, and he flinched, which caused both of the girls to laugh.

"That's funny," Maya observed. "I've never seen a boy so naked or so scared."

"I know, right?" Juliette replied. "I like it. Are you scared, naked boy?" she asked, taunting him some more.

"Yes, Miss," he admitted. It was embarrassing, but true.

The girls laughed, and then Juliette delivered another smack of the paddle across his balls. Again, they watched the expression on his face as he reacted to the pain and embarrassment. And again, it caused them both to laugh.

"I want to hear him say that he likes it," Maya said deviously.

"Oh, interesting," Juliette replied. "Say that you like being spanked across the balls," she demanded, gently tapping his balls with the paddle as she said it.

"Admit it."

Antony took a deep breath.

"I like being spanked across the balls, Miss."

Juliette delivered a particularly hard smack with the paddle. He let out a gasp, followed by a moan, which caused the girls to laugh. His knees went weak for a moment, but again, he managed to remain standing.

"I want to see him on his knees," Maya commented. "I wonder if you need to smack his balls harder."

"That would be fun to find out," Juliette replied. "And as we just heard him say, he likes having his balls spanked, so I think we owe it to him to show him what we can do. And we owe to ourselves to see if we can put him on his knees."

She retrieved from her closet a length of soft nylon rope and made a slipknot in one end. She placed it around Antony's balls and pulled it tight. She handed the other end to Maya and asked her to please hold it tightly, pulling his balls up and forward so that they were defenseless against the wooden paddle.

"Are you ready to be put on your knees?" Juliette asked. "Because we really want to see that happen, and we think you owe it to us to show us that."

He was clearly afraid and turned on at the same time.

"If you want, Miss," he said, his voice trembling.

"Yeah, I want," Juliette replied. "So, we expect you to impress us."

With that, she began to smack him across the balls, not waiting between slaps of the wooden paddle, but delivering one after another in quick succession. After six continuous strokes, he finally fell to his knees, which was received with exultant and victorious laughter from Juliette and Maya.

"He looks so cute when he's on his knees!" Maya cried out.

"I think we should reward him by allowing him to masturbate for us in that position," Juliette replied.

"Absolutely, I think it would be so much more fun to watch him play with himself after having his balls spanked."

Maya handed Juliette the rope leash, saying, "I believe he is *your* property, so you should hold the leash."

"We can share, my love," Juliette said with a wink.

But she took the leash, and as the two girls took a seat on the sofa, she instructed Antony to begin masturbating.

Though Antony had previously felt tremendously exposed and vulnerable, he was now learning an entirely new level of nakedness. Kneeling before Juliette and Maya with his balls on a leash, and masturbating for an audience, made him appreciate a level of embarrassment and intimidation he could not previously have imagined.

"I have an idea," Juliette said, sounding devious.

She stood up and tied the rope leash to the leg of the desk a few feet behind him.

"Get on your hands and knees," she demanded.

When he had complied, she said, "Now crawl forward until the rope is tight."

He crawled forward until the rope pulled tight.

"Now put your hand on your dick, but instead of moving your hand, thrust with your hips," she instructed.

As he began to comply, it was not lost on anyone in the room that with every forward thrust of his hips, the rope leash drew tighter.

"I like how his muscles flex when he thrusts," Maya observed.

"I know. I think maybe he should get a whipping across his butt for that very reason," Juliette replied.

"Oh my God, you're amazing," Maya replied. "That would be so perfect to watch him take a whipping from you. And it makes watching him masturbate so much better, thinking about an impending whipping across his bare butt."

"OK, here's the deal," Juliette stated. "He is allowed to come only if he agrees to take a very thorough whipping."

She knelt down before Antony and asked him directly, "Do you want to come?"

"Yes, Miss," he replied.

"I'm sure you do. So do you agree that you need a whipping?"

"Yes, Miss," he replied.

"Good." She untied the rope leash from the leg of the desk, then said, "Now lie on your back and make yourself come on your chest."

He repositioned himself, and within moments, he began to come. Juliette and Maya observed closely, intrigued by the power of watching him have an orgasm. He came all over his chest, unable to restrain himself in surrendering to the extraordinary pleasure of it.

After they cleaned him off with a towel, they had him return to his hands and knees. Juliette took the leather belt from where Antony's clothing had been discarded and held the two ends in one hand, forming a loop. The belt had a wide, thick leather strap, and it appeared to have the potential to turn his butt red without too much effort.

"Oh, it looks like you are in big trouble," Maya directed at Antony. "It looks like you're about to get what's coming to you."

"That's right. We don't let naked boys come without punishment, do we?" Juliette added.

This made Maya laugh as she agreed, "No, we certainly do not. And he came really hard, so …"

"So, we whip his ass really hard," Juliette said, finishing the thought.

Juliette drew the belt back and began to whip his bare ass with the thick leather strap while Maya watched. She was absolutely fascinated by the sight of a naked boy getting whipped, but even more so by the power to compel a boy to do as he was told.

"Wow," Maya exclaimed, impressed by the sight. "The expression on his face shows a level of devotion to you that's amazing. It's like, the harder you whip him, the more he adores you. I've never seen a boy look so naked," she observed. "And it kind of looks like his dick is getting hard again."

By the time Juliette had turned his rear end a bright red with the belt, Antony had an erection.

"Let's watch him make himself come again," Juliette suggested.

"Absolutely, I think that would be perfect," Maya agreed.

"Please get up on your knees and start playing with yourself," Juliette said to Antony.

Juliette sat on the sofa next to Maya, and the two began to speak openly about the possibilities that were available to them in terms of playing with Antony. They were beginning to imagine all that they might do with him and what fun they could have at his expense.

Snow

The end of the fall semester was quickly approaching. The late-afternoon sunlight streamed down through the treetops, and a couple inches of early-December snow were already on the ground. Emily, Aiden, and Ryan had made the relatively short walk out into the woods behind the school in honor of the first day of snow. Emily couldn't stop smiling at the joyous sight of her two favorite boys, each to one side of her. She found no end to the delight of turning from one to the other and finding them right by her side.

When they arrived at a clearing in the trees, which created a small stage with a wooded backdrop, she came to a stop and looked expectantly at her two companions.

"I think this would be a perfect place," Emily pronounced.

Aiden and Ryan looked around, surveying the location with some trepidation.

"Now take off your sweaters," she said with a big smile. "Slowly," she added, as she brought her camera up to her eye.

They each gave her a look that was a combination of conflicting emotions, and to her, it was like a multilayered decadent dessert. On display for her to enjoy was their lust, their desire, but also their fear. They had yet to learn all that she desired. So, they each crossed their arms to either side, taking hold of their heavy woolen sweaters and pulled them upward.

Every few inches, she had them stop and remain in that position so that she could take a photo.

The fading sunlight, soft and flame colored, glinted along the smooth surface of the snow. Their exposed skin, with what was left of their summer tans, stood out against the paper-white snowy backdrop. She marveled at their never-ending compliance with her demands. It seemed as though anything she asked of them was hers to enjoy the moment the words had left her lips.

"Now take off the rest of your clothes," Emily said.

"Here? In the snow?" Aiden asked.

Ryan looked about, also apparently concerned.

Emily, momentarily perturbed, replied, "Yes, in the snow. You boys won't be wearing anything for the next few hours, at least, so it won't be a problem."

They both took off their pants, and after another look around, began lowering their underwear. They were already getting hard, which was intriguing to Emily.

"Slower," she said as she took a photo.

She was amused by the sight of their cocks bursting out of their underwear as they slid them down. Within moments they had removed the last of their clothing, and she would have been hard-pressed to come up with a time when she had seen anything look so completely naked as her two boys, with their dicks out, completely naked in the snow. It was a sight she was happy to be capturing.

"Those dicks are mine," she murmured to herself as she took another photo.

She slowly surveyed their bodies as she continued to photograph them. She directed them to pose, suggesting positions that would make them look even more exposed. The layer of snow on the ground made the images look magical, and the fact that their dicks were hard made the photos look pornographic. She marveled at their desire to please her, and she observed that the more she challenged them, the more they responded, in a way that made them appear continuously more exposed, and even more naked. Every photo captured this exposure, making it permanent. Every picture advanced and intensified her ownership of them.

The waning late-afternoon sunlight fell across the front of their bodies. She had them pose in what she called "the position," with their arms up and their hands behind their head. Their caramel-colored skin stood in stark contrast to the white snow that surrounded them. She felt something akin to embarrassment at how naked they were, and the context of the situation only served to heighten that appearance. She studied the look on their faces, which displayed quite plainly the manner in which the situation was affecting them. She could see that they were aroused, and that they both desired her in a profound way. She could also see that they were a bit on edge, even nervous to be so exposed for her.

"Place your hands on your cocks for me," she said while keeping her eye on the camera image. "I want to take some photos of you two masturbating."

They held their cocks in their hands, slowly sliding them back and forth. The pleasure of this assignment was evident in their facial expressions, which she captured with her camera. She held the camera down for a moment and watched them masturbate for her.

She then brought the camera up to take another photo. She wanted each image to serve as a document of their desperation and desire for her. Their desire was evident in the intensity of their erections, and their desperation was obvious in the full-frontal display of their naked bodies, as they were offering themselves for her to view.

After she had taken her last photo and led them back to her dorm room, she turned on the shower and waited until the steam from the hot water had fully fogged up the mirror.

"Would you boys care to undress me?" she asked and had to laugh over their enthusiastic response.

When all three of them were naked, she ordered the boys into the hot shower. For the first time, she felt the unbridled desire they both had for her. She turned from one to the other, kissing them, touching them, and feeling their hands all over her body. She had one hand on Aiden and the other on Ryan. It surprised her to learn how similar their bodies felt, yet she was delighted to discover all the little differences between them. She had

Aiden in front of her, kissing her, while Ryan stood behind her, his hands on her breasts as he kissed the back of her neck. She could feel Ryan's erect cock on her butt and lower back, and she could feel Aiden's cock against her belly. She slid her hands down the front of their bodies and was thrilled to wrap her hands around both of her boys' cocks simultaneously.

When she invited them both into her bed, she felt as though, for the first time, she had what she wanted. The attention she felt from both her lovers, each focused on electrifying her body with previously unknown pleasures, was exactly what was she had desired, but had never known would be available to her. She didn't need to decide since she could have both. They weren't jealous of each other, but they both wanted her to know how much they adored her and were somewhat competitive in showering her with affection. And so it didn't matter who made her come and which of them came inside of her, as they were both of equal standing in her eyes, and they knew it. All they wanted was to belong to her.

The Party

One of the traditions at the Academy was the party that marked the end of the fall semester. It would be the last time all of the students would be together before the winter break, and the school tended to go all out for the event. It was held in the main gallery, where there was champagne, hors d'oeuvres, and a DJ playing dance music. All of the students were happy to have completed the semester and appreciated the opportunity to let loose a bit before going home for the holidays.

"James, I want you to lick my pussy," Madison whispered as they stood on the balcony overlooking the gallery.

James looked at her in wonderment. She was so forward, but he loved it. He smiled, then kissed her, then slowly sank to his knees before her. He slid her dress upward, leaning in to kiss her between her legs before he even removed her panties.

Madison leaned back against the railing, her legs spread just enough to allow his tongue to slip between her thighs and caress her clit. She was, as always, impressed by the length of his tongue, and the creativity with which he used it, but she was perhaps even more impressed by the devotion with which he served her and pleasured her. She was amused by the thought that someone might show up at any moment. The fact that James appeared concerned only with kneeling and licking her pussy was impressive to her, since she knew that he was nervous about being discovered in such a compromising position. She decided that he would lick her for as long as she wanted, but after twenty minutes or so, she placed her hand on the back of his head and motioned for him to stand up.

"More later," she said appreciatively. "Now let's go get a drink and mark the end of this semester in style."

Sarah found Charlotte standing at one end of the main gallery, observing the crowd of students, and handed her a drink.

"Is that Ms. Harwood standing over there, and is she actually holding her fucking birch rod?" Charlotte asked incredulously.

"I believe that it is, which is just about perfect. It's like she's playing her character. Hilarious," Sarah replied.

At that moment, Richard walked by, and Sarah grabbed him.

"Hey, Dick. I want you to walk over to Ms. Harwood and tell her that you just can't finish the semester without one last taste of her birch rod."

"No, please, Miss, I can't!" Dick protested.

"Did you just say, you *can't?*" Because if you don't, then I'll tell the dean that you were masturbating in the shower room."

Dick's eyes clouded over with fear.

"No! Please?! You know what would happen if you did that!"

"Yeah, Dick, I know exactly what would happen, which is why you are going to go have a little conversation with Ms. Harwood."

Dick looked like a lost puppy as he slowly turned and walked toward Ms. Harwood.

"That was fucking awesome," Charlotte said. "You are the best."

"I know, I totally am."

One of the delightful touches to the party was Ms. Strickland's latest photo work, which was a retelling of "The Three Little Pigs." It was displayed along one wall of the main gallery. The other wall contained a selection of student works. Emily was proud to see that not only had a few of her photos been selected, but also, both Aiden and Ryan were represented in her work.

"My God, Emily, these are amazing photos! You have talent!" Madison said in earnest.

"Oh, thank you. I'm just really happy to see both of my boys up on the wall. I think they look good, right?"

Ryan and Aiden stood on either side of her, an unmistakable look of pride on their faces.

"Yeah, Emily. You and your gorgeous boys. I should hire you to photograph James and his magnificent cock ... as long as you don't decide that you are so greedy that you need three boys for your stable."

Emily laughed.

"Of course, I would take photos for you, but I certainly wouldn't charge you. And no, three is too many. I only have room for one on each side," she said to Madison with a wink, pulling her two boys close to her.

Later in the evening Emily caught the eye of David from her photography class, and as always, he tensed up when he saw her.

"Relax, David," she said with a reassuring smile. "I only busted your balls the one time. The chance of that happening again is, well, likely, but it isn't going to happen tonight."

She laughed as he swallowed hard, his eyes wide with fear.

"Anyway, even though you were wearing a mask, I could tell it was you who Ms. Strickland enlisted for her 'Three Little Pigs' photo series. You were one of the pigs, right?"

"Yes, Miss. I had the house made of sticks," he offered.

"Well, you looked really naked and objectified. I mean, it's totally embarrassing for you, but I very much liked it."

"Thank you, Miss. I, um, appreciate that," David replied, still looking nervous.

"Not a problem. One question, though: When the wolf woman has captured all three little pigs and she has them strung up in her house, it looks like she slams her knee into your balls really hard. How did Ms. Strickland achieve that effect?"

David looked at Emily as if he might cry.

"She had the model who was playing the wolf woman slam her knee into my balls."

"Hmmm. So, was it just the once?"

"No, Miss. It was, ah … many, many times."

Juliette, Maya, and Antony entered the party and quickly found Charlotte and Sarah.

"Hey, girls. What's happening?" Juliette asked.

Charlotte and Sarah raised their cups.

"Hey, you three," Charlotte greeted them. She then gave Antony a quick look up and down and cried out in surprise when she noticed two feet of thin red nylon cord that led from the waist of Antony's pants to Juliette's hand.

"Is that, um, connected to anything?" Charlotte inquired.

"Yeah, it's tied around his dick," Juliette replied with a laugh. "But you really have to see it, because it's more complicated than that. Let me show you."

Juliette unbuttoned Antony's pants and drew down the zipper, exposing the waistband of his charcoal-gray boxer briefs. She lifted her hand up to his shoulder, pulling the nylon cord tight. This caused his dick to pop out of his underwear as though she were puppeteering it. Charlotte laughed at the novelty of the arrangement. It wasn't as though any of the party's attendees would particularly mind if they noticed what was happening, but it was a remarkable sight, nonetheless. Juliette held the cord like a leash, which pulled Antony's dick upward and exposed another, much shorter length of cord, which was tied around his dick as well as his balls. The length of this cord prevented his dick from becoming fully erect, as it forced it into a "U" shape.

"Does it hurt?" Charlotte inquired.

Antony noted that she was asking Juliette, not him.

"No, not really," Juliette responded. "I mean, it's tight, for sure, and I'll make him wear it all night, so it will be a relief for him when Maya and I finally untie it. But otherwise," she continued as she emphasized her words by jiggling the cord, making his dick and balls bounce, "he is totally fine."

"Well, I have to say that it's ingenious and totally cute," Charlotte said. "I have never seen a cock tied up like that. So, what happens if he gets hard?"

Maya laughed.

"Good question!" she replied with a wicked smile on her face. "What do you think, Antony? Do you want to show Charlotte how big your dick is? You want to make it big and hard for us?" She winked at Charlotte to let her know she was just teasing him.

"The cord is tied to his balls, so the harder he gets, the more it pulls, and the tighter it gets," Juliette explained. "So, he can't get completely hard. It's really frustrating for him, but that's where all the fun is. He wants to get hard, but then he *doesn't* want to. It's quite a predicament for him. And the harder he gets, the more he is forced into this lovely bow shape."

Again, she emphasized the curve of his shaft with her index finger, tracing a line from the base to the tip.

"Do you mind if I take a photo of it?" Sarah asked.

"Of course you can take a photo," Juliette replied.

Sarah pulled her phone out of her purse and took a few photos. The brief flashes drew some attention, but no one decided to bother them or intrude upon their evening.

At this point, Antony began to pull his pants back up, thinking that the girls were done with their investigation of the way in which he was tied up.

"Stop," Juliette said, somewhat surprised. "What do you think you're doing?"

"I just thought that ..." Antony began.

"We're not done," Maya said. "We will tell you when we're done. So, pants down."

Antony complied, sliding them back down. Juliette gave the little leash a yank to admonish him. This caused his dick to bounce again, which made Charlotte laugh. She was still fascinated by the fact that his private parts were tied up, and even more by the fact he was being made to display this potentially embarrassing situation. Because it amused her so, Juliette offered her the leash.

"Would you care to see what it's like? I promise you, it's fun."

"Absolutely!"

Charlotte took the leash in her hand, pulling it this way and that, observing how it made Antony's dick bounce back and forth in response.

"The cord that's tied to his balls is really tight," she observed. "And from the size of him, I guess he's pretty hard right now."

Juliette laughed.

"Oh, he gets a lot harder than that," Maya added.

A girl named Olivia, accompanied by a boy named Daniel, approached Charlotte and Sarah and asked, "You two created The Book, right?"

"Yeah, we did," Charlotte replied. "Why?"

"I just wanted to thank you." She gestured to the guy she had with her and added, "I got this guy because of it."

"Well, that's totally cool," Sarah commented. "And what was it that worked for you?" she asked, always looking to improve the functionality of the site for its users.

"I have this, uh, little obsession," Olivia claimed, "So I wanted a cute guy with a tiny dick. I've had some disappointments. So, I met Daniel, who does, in fact, have a tiny dick."

Charlotte laughed, and said, "Yeah, we kind of couldn't believe it when we saw it. I think he has the tiniest dick of all the guys at the Academy."

"Yes!" Olivia exclaimed. "And I *love* how tiny it is!"

Daniel wore an expression that revealed both embarrassment and pride, as Olivia pulled him close and kissed him on the cheek.

"Well, we're glad that works for you," Sarah replied.

Olivia paused, sensing that she was being misunderstood.

"Oh, wait, no—my boyfriend is really well hung," Olivia explained. "Daniel here lets me indulge my fascination with humiliating a guy who has a tiny, little dick," she said, laughing. "It only works for me if he has tiny balls too, and this guy," she said as she reached between Daniel's legs and gave him a squeeze, "has such a teeny, tiny package!"

Olivia laughed, and Charlotte and Sarah couldn't help but also be amused. Daniel's face blushed bright red, and Olivia seemed to be soaking up every delicious drop of his humiliation.

"Are you going to show me Mr. Tiny later on tonight so I can laugh at it?" she whispered into Daniel's ear.

"If you like, Miss," Daniel replied.

Olivia kissed him on the cheek, feeling the intense heat of his embarrassment on her lips.

"Wow," Charlotte murmured, watching Olivia and Daniel disappear into the crowded party. "I feel so proud to have been a part of something remarkable. I think we did a really beautiful thing."

"Absolutely," Sarah replied. "And I credit myself for creating the feature that allows people to search the database by dick size."

Charlotte laughed.

"Yeah, that part was genius. It's weird that I don't know this, but who has the biggest dick?" she asked.

"Really? You never found out for yourself? Because he's coming straight toward us."

At that moment, Madison and James approached.

"Hey, ladies. Happy end of semester!" Madison offered, raising her glass.

Emily appeared moments later with Aiden and Ryan in tow.

"I'm really looking forward to next semester," Emily observed.

"Oh, really," Madison replied, looking amused. "Is it the academically rigorous coursework that you are looking forward to?"

Emily couldn't miss the irony dripping from Madison's question.

"Ha-ha, OK. No, it's not that," Emily admitted with a laugh. She paused, smiling and feeling appreciative of her new best friend, Madison. "I'm looking forward to what we get to do to the boys," she said with a broad smile, as she and Madison toasted the end of their first semester at the Academy.

Printed in Great Britain
by Amazon